Claiming the Single Mom's Heart

Glynna Kaye

HARLEQUIN® LOVE INSPIRED®

Recycling programs for this product may not exist in your area.

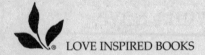 LOVE INSPIRED BOOKS

ISBN-13: 978-0-373-71953-2

Claiming the Single Mom's Heart

www.Harlequin.com

Printed in U.S.A.

"Hey! How is everybody this morning?"

Her heart inexplicably lifting at the sound of the familiar voice, Sunshine turned to see Grady striding toward them with that distinctive masculine gait, his impossibly broad shoulders clad in a windbreaker.

"Grady!" To Sunshine's surprise, her daughter let out a cry of welcome and abandoned the swing to run toward him.

When Tessa reached Grady, she grabbed his hand and gazed happily up at him. "Now you can see how high I can swing."

He glanced at Sunshine, looking slightly taken aback at Tessa's grip on his hand. "I can do that."

Willingly, he allowed her to pull him forward to stand next to her mother.

Tessa dashed for the swings. In a flash, she had herself moving.

"Are you watching?" a demanding voice called.

"We're watching!" they yelled in unison, then exchanged a glance and laughed.

The kindergartner was pumping herself higher and higher, a determined look on her little face.

"You're doing great, Tessa!" Grady's words of encouragement impelled her to pump harder, and her triumphant smile widened.

Sunshine's heart swelled with love.

Glynna Kaye treasures memories of growing up in small Midwestern towns—and vacations spent with the Texan side of the family. She traces her love of storytelling to the times a houseful of great-aunts and great-uncles gathered with her grandma to share candid, heartwarming, poignant and often humorous tales of their youth and young adulthood. Glynna now lives in Arizona, where she enjoys gardening, photography and the great outdoors.

"For I know the plans I have for you," declares the Lord, "plans to prosper you and not to harm you, plans to give you hope and a future."
—*Jeremiah* 29:11

The Lord Himself goes before you and will be with you; He will never leave you nor forsake you. Do not be afraid; do not be discouraged.
—*Deuteronomy* 31:8

To Jim and Phyllis Dorman, whose deep love of God and faithful ministry have greatly influenced my life. Thank you.

Chapter One

"A family legend is worthless unless you have proof."

"I'm going to get proof." With more confidence than she felt, Sunshine Carston gave her longtime friend Tori a reassuring nod. "It's just taking longer than expected."

Much longer.

She shifted restlessly in the passenger seat of Victoria Janner's steel-blue Kia compact as they searched for a parking spot in the crowded graveled lot of Hunter's Hideaway. Her own ancient SUV was in the shop—again—and out-of-town visitor Tori had agreed to take a detour while running errands Saturday morning. But Tori's willingness had swiftly evaporated when on the way to their destination Sunshine had divulged her true intention for this next stop.

Big mistake.

She rolled down her window, breathing in the soothing scent of sun-warmed ponderosa pines. An aroma deliciously indigenous to the rugged mountain country surrounding Hunter Ridge, Arizona, it was one her great-great-grandparents would have been familiar with. One she herself would have likely grown up with had life not dealt her ancestors an unfair blow.

She stared across the parking lot at the connecting log, stone and frame structures that made up the main building of Hunter's Hideaway. The vast wooded acreage had been a home away from home for hunters, horsemen, hikers and other outdoorsmen since Harrison "Duke" Hunter had—allegedly—rooted it to that exact spot early in the past century.

"*They* seem to be doing a good business this Labor Day weekend." Resentment welled up within her. "No noisy remodeling like they're inflicting on the Artists' Cooperative gallery this morning."

A cute blonde with a pixie haircut, Tori and her usual dazzling smile was nowhere to be seen as they slipped into an empty spot. "If you go in there with a chip on your shoulder," she cautioned, "you can't expect a positive outcome."

What response had Sunshine hoped to get from her friend when she'd confessed her true motive for relocating to Hunter Ridge two years ago? A cry of outrage at the unfairness of it all? Reinforcement of her plans? Encouragement to face her fear of the influential family who the town was named for?

"And don't forget," Tori added as she cut off the engine, "what the good Lord says about revenge."

"I'm seeking justice. Not revenge. There's a difference."

A *big* difference. Revenge involved retaliation. Inflicting injury. Justice had to do with revealing truth and righting wrongs. And yes, restoring of at least some of what by rights belonged to her family. To her. And to her five-year-old daughter, Tessa.

Tori cast her a disbelieving look. "Surely you don't think anyone is going to fork over restitution for something your great-great-grandfather was supposedly cheated out of. Even if you could prove it—which I doubt you can—you don't have the money to back up your claim with legal action."

"No, but I'm counting on the seemingly impeccable reputation of the Hunters to apply its own brand of pressure. That they'll be compelled, for the sake of their standing in the community, to make things right once the facts are brought to their attention."

Tori slumped down in the bucket seat. "I wish you hadn't told me any of this. It sounds too much like blackmail."

Sunshine made a face. "Not blackmail. I look at it as an opportunity for them to live up to their good name. I don't hold it against later generations that Duke Hunter didn't play well with others."

"You could get hauled into court if one of them thinks it smacks of extortion." Tori gave her a sharp glance. "Especially now that you've decided to run for a town council seat against one of the family members."

Against Elaine Hunter, who was trying for a second term.

"Everything will be aboveboard. Trust me, okay?"

If only her maternal grandmother, Alice Heywood, were still alive. She'd recall the details of the account Sunshine remembered hearing as a kid. The vague references to "the ridge of the hunter." A betrayal by someone considered a friend. It was a story, though, which over time she'd dismissed as nothing but a fairy tale that once captured her childish imagination. That was, until her world turned upside down not long after her daughter's birth and she began pondering the possibilities.

"The din from their renovation of the property next to the Artists' Co-op," she continued, "offers a perfect excuse for a visit. You heard the racket this morning. That less-than-sympathetic contractor overseeing the project told me to take it up with the Hunters. So here I am."

Squaring her shoulders, she'd just exited the vehicle when someone stepped out on the covered porch that stretched across the front of the adjoined buildings. A muscle in her midsection involuntarily tightened.

"Oh, no, not *him*," she whispered. Wouldn't you know it? That too-handsome-for-his-own-good Grady Hunter, cell phone pressed to his ear, now paced the length of the porch like a lion guarding the entrance to his lair.

Although she'd only seen him around town, she'd heard plenty of starry-eyed feminine gossip surrounding the popular ladies' man. Having once had a personal, close-up view of what it was like to be married to a male with that reputation, she wasn't impressed.

"I wanted to get invited inside to talk to his mom or his grandma so I could look around. You know, for clues. But I don't want to deal with this guy."

"Maybe God doesn't think snooping is a good idea," Tori said.

"I have to start somewhere, don't I?" She focused again on the broad-shouldered man striding across the porch. Black trousers. Snow-white shirt. Gray vest. Black bow tie.

"Why's he dressed like that?" Tori echoed the question forming in Sunshine's mind.

Then realization dawned and any remaining courage to take on the Hunters drained out of her. "I forgot. It's his older brother's wedding day."

How had she lost track of such a high-profile event? Widower and single dad Luke Hunter was marrying Delaney Marks, a young woman who Sunshine had become acquainted with over the past summer. Obviously she'd been way too busy and much too preoccupied if she'd forgotten. So what was new?

"Maybe you'd better come back in a few days." Tori sounded relieved that her mission might be aborted.

"But by then the holiday weekend will be over, the last of the summer customers come and gone." There might soon be leaf-peepers searching for a burst of aspen gold—and hunters, of course—but the prime season to market the talents of local artists would be over until late next spring. "I have a responsibility to represent the best interests of our artists' community. And that constant din next door isn't one of them."

Torn, she again looked to where Grady had finished his conversation and pocketed his cell phone. She found big, self-confident men intimidating, but she'd have no choice but to deal with him if she ventured forth now.

Intruding on a family gathering, though, might not be the best strategy. Nor would stating the case for the Artists' Co-op to the man on the porch rather than to his civic-minded mother. But before she could get back in the car, Grady's gaze swept the parking lot and he spotted her, his eyes locking on hers.

Her heart jerked as his expression appeared to sharpen. Question. Challenge.

The decision was made.

"Ramp up the prayers, Tori." She shut the car door, cutting off her friend's words of protest. *Here we go, Lord.*

What was *she* doing here?

Grady Hunter's eyes narrowed as the petite young woman, her black hair glinting in the late-morning sunlight, wove her way between cars in the parking lot. Clad in jeans and a black T-shirt, the fringe of her camel-colored jacket swaying with each step, Sunshine Carston looked like one determined woman.

Just what he didn't need right now. Not, for that matter, what any of the Hunter clan needed while setting aside anxious thoughts regarding his mother's recent cancer diagnosis in order to celebrate today. Couldn't whatever Sunshine had on her mind wait until after the Labor Day weekend? Or at least until after the guests dispersed from his big brother's postwedding brunch, which was now in full swing?

Having ditched his tux jacket inside, he loosened his tie, regretting having stepped outside for a breath of fresh air and to make a quick phone call. He didn't know who Ms. Carston intended to see, but regardless he would halt her at the door. Admittedly, he had a reputation for being overly protective of his family. But thirty-four years of life's lessons had given him reason to be, and today would be no different.

"Good morning." An almost shy smile accompanied her greeting as she paused at the base of the porch steps, but her dark brown eyes reflected the resolve he'd initially identified from a distance.

Up close she was prettier than he'd originally thought from seeing her around town and—only recently—in church. Although his area of expertise was wildlife photography, he nonetheless found himself mentally framing her for a perfect shot. Not a stiffly formal studio portrait, though. She was far too vibrant for that.

Her glossy, shoulder-length hair, slightly longer in front than in back, accented her straight nose and high cheekbones, and a smooth, warm skin tone hinted of possible Native American ancestry. She appeared to be in her late twenties—much too young to challenge his mother or Irvin Baydlin for a seat on the town council.

From what he'd heard from multiple sources—including his mom—she kept the current council members on their toes. Which, of course, wasn't necessarily a bad thing.

But he wouldn't be voting for her.

"Good morning," he acknowledged with a friendly nod. Hunters were known for their hospitality, and he'd uphold that to his dying day or risk repercussions from Grandma Jo. He stepped off the porch and extended his hand. "Grady Hunter. How may I help you?"

Doe-like eyes met his in momentary hesitation, and then she gripped his hand in a firm shake. "Sunshine Carston. Manager of the Hunter Ridge Artists' Cooperative."

Her voice was softer, gentler, than he'd assumed from her reputation. That, combined with the delicate hand she'd placed in his, contradicted the image he'd previously formed of the single mom as "one tough cookie."

She motioned to the overflowing parking lot of the property his great-great-grandparents had settled in the early 1900s. "I apologize for the intrusion. I forgot this is Delaney Marks's wedding day."

That was right, his brother's new bride was, coincidentally, an aspiring artist herself and, in exchange for jewelry-making lessons from another local artist, on occasion worked at the Artists' Co-op.

"I won't take but a few minutes of your time," she said, not waiting to see if he'd voice any objections to conducting business on his brother's wedding day. "The adjoining property north of the Artists' Co-op is being renovated by a contractor hired by Hunter Enterprises."

"That's correct."

"I realize Hunter's Hideaway caters to a different customer base," she continued, and he found himself drawn to the softly lilting voice, the expressive eyes. "But, as a fellow business owner who is impacted by visitors to this region, you know how important the months from Memorial Day weekend through Labor Day are to local businesses."

"They are indeed." Fortunately, although Hunter's Hideaway no longer offered guided hunts on their own property or in the neighboring national forests, they'd diversified through the years to not only provide camping and cabins for hunters, but also for competitive trail riders and runners seeking to condition at a higher altitude. For seekers of a quiet place to get away from it all, as well.

Those more recent additions, in fact, gave him hope that he might soon see his long-held dream come to fruition—wildlife-photography workshops and related guided tours of the forested wilderness surrounding them. But he had to convince his family that it was worthwhile. Not an easy thing to do.

Sunshine's dark eyes pinned him. "Then, you can understand how sales might be negatively impacted at a fine-arts gallery when the adjoining property is undergoing a massive overhaul on the last holiday weekend of the season."

So that was the problem. It couldn't be that bad, though, could it? It wasn't as if they were dynamiting. "No harm intended, I assure you."

"The contractor overseeing the project says he's under a tight deadline." She folded her arms as she looked up at him. "We've had disgruntled customers walk out of the gallery when the pounding, vibration and whine of power tools wouldn't let up."

Weighing his options, he briefly stared at formidable clouds building in the distance for what would likely bring an afternoon monsoon rain. "What do you say I give the contractor a call and postpone things for a few days? I imagine he and his crew wouldn't mind having the rest of the weekend off."

Brows arched as if in disbelief. Or was that disappointment flickering through her eyes? Had she expected— relished even—a fight?

"You'd do that?"

"Neighbors have to look out for neighbors."

The contractor did have a deadline, but there was no point in making things harder for Grady's mother right now by waving a red flag in Ms. Carston's face. Although the family was struggling to come to terms with Mom's upcoming surgery—a single-side mastectomy—she insisted she still intended to run for office, so there was no point in riling up one of her opponents unnecessarily.

"Well, then…" Sunshine's uncertain tone betrayed that verbalizing gratitude wasn't easy for her in this instance, almost as if she suspected she'd missed something in their exchange. That maybe he was trying to pull a fast one on her. "Thank you, Mr. Hunter."

"Grady. And you're welcome."

But she didn't depart. Instead, she stood looking at him almost expectantly.

"Was there something else?"

An unexpected smile surfaced. "I'm waiting for you to make the call."

Oh, she was, was she?

A smile of his own tugged in response to the one that had made his breath catch, and he pulled out his cell phone. He wasn't used to not being trusted to do what he said he'd do. But anything to keep the peace, right? And to keep Sunshine smiling like that. On Mom's behalf, of course.

Under her watchful gaze he put some distance between them, then punched the contractor's speed-dial number. "Ted. It's Grady. I hear you've got your crew working this weekend."

"A deadline's a deadline," the gravelly voice responded, his tone defensive. "I've never missed one yet."

"That work ethic is certainly why you were picked for the job." Grady cut a look at Sunshine. "But what do you say we extend it by a week and let you and your boys knock off for the rest of the holiday weekend?"

It would be cutting it close, but an extra week wouldn't be a deal breaker, would it?

After a long pause, Ted chuckled. "That pretty artist complained to you, didn't she?"

Grady forced a smile as he nodded reassuringly in Sunshine's direction. "You're welcome, Ted."

"Pushover."

Was he? "Glad I could help your crew out."

The contractor chuckled again. "Be careful there, Grady. You're playing with fire."

"Sure thing. You have a good one, too, bud."

Pocketing his cell phone again, Grady moved back to Sunshine. "All done."

From the wary look in her eyes, she clearly hadn't anticipated he'd willingly accommodate her. A sense of satisfaction rose, catching her off guard, throwing a wrench in her assumptions.

"Anything else?" He needed to get back inside. They'd be cutting the cake shortly and he'd promised a toast. "I know you'd once approached Hunter Enterprises about leasing the property next door to expand the Artists' Co-op, but we've long had plans for it. We'll do our best to be a top-notch neighbor."

"It's true we could use the additional space, but it will be nice having a bookstore in town."

He frowned. "Bookstore?"

"You're opening a bookstore, right?"

"No."

"I heard it was going to be a bookstore."

"It's not."

"Then, what—" her words came cautiously, reflecting a growing dread in her eyes "—will be going in next door to us?"

Chapter Two

"Hunter Ridge Wild Game Supply."

"When you say *wild game*," Sunshine ventured without much hope, "I don't suppose you mean a place that sells video games?"

Laugh lines crinkled at the corners of Grady's deep blue eyes and she steeled herself against the engaging grin. This was Grady Hunter, ladies' man, and she'd do well to keep that in mind. He'd been unexpectedly accommodating about the renovation next door. What was he up to?

"No, I mean a store that sells equipment and supplies for processing wild game. You know, stuff for making elk sausage and venison steaks."

Okay. Deep breath. She could handle this. Her great-great-grandfather had, according to her grandmother, been a marksman who'd put food on the table with his hunting skills. She herself wasn't any more squeamish about wild game than she was about buying chicken or a pound of hamburger at the grocery store. But some Co-op members might disagree.

"Not solely in-store sales, but online, as well," Grady continued, a note of pride in his voice. "Once we pass inspection, we'll also be officially licensed to do processing demonstrations as well as process game donated for regional food pantry programs. That's what the ongoing renovation is about—to put in a commercial kitchen, freezers, the works."

She stiffened. *Processing on the premises?* Services that meant hunters hauling their field-dressed trophies through the front door? On the other hand, how could she object to feeding the hungry?

She must have hesitated a moment too long, for Grady's eyes narrowed.

"You have a problem with that?"

Not wanting to give the impression she was opposed to the idea, she offered what she hoped was a convincing smile. As a candidate for town council, she had to weigh her words carefully. It wouldn't be wise, two months before an election, to give the majority of those living in a town catering to outdoorsmen the impression she had issues with that.

She glanced toward the parking lot where Tori was no doubt watching and wondering what was taking her so long. "I personally have no problem with it, but some gallery customers and Co-op members may."

"That's unfortunate." He didn't look concerned. "But your worries are unfounded. We won't hang carcasses in the window or mount a deer head over the front door. It will be low-key. Discreet."

"You do understand my problem, though, don't you?" She looked to him in appeal. "Our members are trying to create a welcoming atmosphere for shoppers of the fine arts. The gulf between the two worlds might be disconcerting for some."

"I know a number of hunters who appreciate the fine arts and who, in fact, are award-winning painters and sculptors of wildlife. Maybe the Co-op should expand its horizons and find a way to better serve the foundation that Hunter Ridge was built on."

"Taxidermy?" She flashed a smile. "I don't think that would go over well with local artists who call this town home."

"Then, it sounds as if folks should have researched Hunter Ridge more closely before coming here, doesn't it?" He quirked a persuasive smile of his own. "You *could* move the gallery, you know. If not to another town, there are empty buildings that I imagine would be suitable."

"Unfortunately..." Sunshine drew in a resigned breath "...the Co-op recently signed a three-year lease."

Which had been her doing. She'd been proud of convincing their out-of-town landlord, Charlotte Gyles, to give the Co-op a lower monthly rental rate in exchange for committing to a three-year contract. But look where it had landed them now. Member Gideon Edlow, who'd give anything to unseat her as manager of the Co-op, would gleefully cry, "I told you so." Being booted out of the position would mean losing the apartment above the gallery and being forced out of town before she'd had a chance to verify her grandmother's story.

She couldn't allow that to happen.

"Even if relocation isn't an option, you don't have anything to worry about." Grady tugged at his loosened tie, and she couldn't help but wonder how he'd looked in the full regalia at that morning's nuptials. "This is to be an unobtrusive, word-of-mouth and online operation. We have a good-size customer base of hunters who have been asking for this type of service for years. Word will get around without fanfare."

She couldn't help but laugh. "That's what I'm afraid of, Mr. Hunter. Word getting around."

"Grady, remember?" Twinkling eyes held her gaze a bit too long. "There's no cause for worry."

Easy enough for him to say. She'd taken a huge risk coming to Hunter Ridge in pursuit of the truth of her grandmother's tale and in accepting the nomination to run for town council on behalf of the artist community.

"Everything will be fine," he concluded. "Trust me."

Trust a Hunter? Like her great-great-grandfather had? Like she'd trusted her ex-husband to stick around after Tessa's birth? "I guess we don't have a choice, do we? That is, unless *you're* willing to relocate?"

Startled brows raised, then his eyes warmed as if charmed by her impertinence. "Not a chance, Sunshine. But if it would put your mind at rest, why don't you come out to the Hideaway this week and take a look at the architectural drawings. I think you'll be satisfied with what you see."

He was inviting her to Hunter's Hideaway?

It wasn't likely that he'd spread the blueprints out on a picnic table under the trees or on the porch, was it? Surely she'd be welcomed beyond the public areas and into the more private ones?

A ripple of excitement danced through her. Right when she'd almost given up hope of a closer look at the property, Grady had unknowingly opened the door to an answered prayer.

She nodded, hoping a carefully casual response wouldn't betray her eagerness. "If I can find the time, I might do that."

"Don't tell me you're thinking of making more changes to those plans, Grady."

With a grin, he looked up from where he'd spread the blueprints across the heavy oak table he used as an office desk. Her silver-gray hair upswept and secured with decorative combs, eighty-year-old Grandma Jo stepped into his office. It wouldn't be long before her signature summertime attire of jeans and a collared shirt gave way to wool slacks and a turtleneck.

"No, no more changes. Sunshine Carston went into a tailspin when she found out we're opening a wild game supply next to the Artists' Co-op." She'd have probably freaked out had he mentioned bow hunters were currently combing neighboring forests for mule deer and that elk season was getting underway. "I made the mistake of inviting her to look at the plans and see for herself that she has nothing to worry about. She called a while ago to say she's on her way."

"That sounds proactive. Why is inviting her here a mistake?"

"Just is," he said with a shrug. He wouldn't admit to his grandmother that the manager of the Artists' Co-op had been on his mind more than she should be. "I guess by going this extra mile to disarm her fears, I almost feel as if I'm fraternizing with the enemy. I mean, she *is* Mom's opponent."

"Nonsense, Grady." Grandma joined him to gaze down at the blueprints. "I have the utmost confidence in you as a guardian of this family's best interests. Don't let that previous situation you found yourself in undermine you. We all make mistakes, and trust those who aren't worthy of our trust. But don't let that weigh on you. Nothing came of it."

Except his own broken heart and the humiliation of the betrayal. Not to mention letting down Jasmine's daughter when things had fallen apart, and how he'd unwittingly risked his family's reputation. *Don't forget that, Grandma.* He hadn't.

Since Hunter had grown up on stories of how his great-great-grandfather had almost lost the Hideaway due to misplaced trust, and seeing with his own eyes the repercussions of Aunt Charlotte's nasty divorce from Dad's younger brother, you'd have thought he'd have been more cautious about where he placed his heart. But he'd been head over heels for Jasmine—who'd falsely given others the impression that he and his family endorsed a controversial land-development project she was orchestrating behind the scenes. One that, had she succeeded, would have resulted in filling her pockets with a lucrative kickback. Thankfully, the ring was still in his pocket when everything came to light. But it had been a close call.

"Grady?" His twenty-year-old sister, Rio, appeared in the doorway, sun-streaked blond hair cascading down her back and her expression troubled. "Sunshine Carston's here. She says you're expecting her, but I asked them to have a seat while I tracked you down."

"Them?" Sunshine brought someone else along? He hadn't counted on a third party.

"Her kid is with her."

Tensed muscles relaxed. "Thanks, I'll go get her in a minute."

Rio departed and Grandma Jo returned to the door.

"This is a smart move, Grady, to put Sunshine's fears to rest. Don't let the past cause you to second-guess yourself."

But had his motive for inviting her been entirely untainted? Since that last disaster in the romance department, he'd rededicated himself to safeguarding the Hunter clan in both business and personal dealings—going to excessive lengths to ensure he didn't make the same mistake again. But had his invitation, ostensibly on behalf of family business, been influenced by a subconscious hope of spending time with the attractive woman?

Now alone in the room, he moved to the window facing the forest behind the Hideaway and adjusted the wooden louvers. Rearranged a chair. Straightened a crooked lampshade.

Then, tamping down an inexplicable sense of anticipation, he paused again to appraise the room—and uttered a silent prayer that his spiritual armor would remain securely in place.

"Come sit by me, sweetheart." Sunshine patted the leather sofa cushion next to her, relieved that Tessa seemed less clingy this morning than she'd been in recent weeks. She'd slept somewhat better last night, too, only calling twice for her to banish something lurking in the shadows of her closet. Now enthralled with the animal heads on the log walls, the half-barrel end tables and an antler-designed chandelier above, it was almost too much to expect her raven-haired kindergartner to anchor herself to one spot.

Maybe she should have waited to come until after Tessa was in school for the afternoon. Having a five-year-old in tow wouldn't make sleuthing for clues easy. But after the holiday weekend, Tori had had to make a quick trip back to the thriving Arizona artists' community of Jerome. Then she'd return tomorrow to help with Tessa and, somewhat reluctantly, with the historic record research Sunshine intended to do.

"Look, Mommy." Tessa pointed to a wide staircase that ascended to an open-railed landing. "Can I go up there?"

"I'm afraid not. We're not guests."

But how tempting to look the other way while Tessa

wandered up the carpeted flight, then hurry up behind her to bring her back, giving herself a chance to look around. This building, of course, may not have existed at the time her great-great-grandparents had been here. Probably hadn't. But could there still be something of value to lend credence to Sunshine's grandma's stories?

"Good morning," a familiar male voice greeted. "I'm glad you could make it here today."

She stared into Grady's smiling eyes as he approached from a hallway beyond the staircase, looking at home in the rustic surroundings. In jeans, work boots and a Western-cut shirt, he exuded a commanding confidence.

She rose from the sofa, a betraying flutter in her stomach. But was that at the prospect of exploring private areas of the historic building? Or spending time with Grady? "I hope you don't mind that I brought my daughter. She won't be in school until this afternoon."

"No problem." Still smiling, he held out his hand to the little girl. "Hi, I'm Grady. What's your name?"

"Tessa." She shyly shook his hand.

"Beautiful name for a beautiful young lady." Grady looked over at Sunshine. "She looks like you."

Sunshine's face warmed. She'd heard that comment before. She'd wildly, foolishly, loved Tessa's father, Jerrel Carston. But she was grateful not to look into a miniversion of his face on a daily basis.

"Is this your house?" Tessa asked, again drawing Grady's attention.

"This is where I do business. I live in a cabin not far from here." He glanced at Sunshine. "Would you like to come back to my office? I can walk you through the plans."

"Thank you. Come on, Tessa."

They followed Grady through a shadowed hallway,

Sunshine taking her time as she tried to absorb everything around her. Old photographs, paintings and sketches on the walls. An antique mirror. Faded framed embroidery work.

Up ahead Grady waited outside an open door, watching as she paused to study the faces in one of the yellowing photos.

"Is this your family?"

He laughed, and the sound unexpectedly warmed her. "Who knows? Mom's been known to rescue historic photographs from garage sales and antique shops, and they can pop up anywhere—guest rooms, cabins, hallways."

Disappointed, she gave the image a lingering look as Grady beckoned her and Tessa forward to usher them into his office.

Inside the sunlit room, he motioned for them to take a seat off to the side, his gaze touching apologetically on her daughter. "I'm afraid I don't have any fun kid stuff, Tessa."

But as always, Tessa's eyes were wide, taking in her surroundings with interest. The book-lined shelves, wall groupings of photographs from an earlier era and striking black-and-white photos of wildlife. Elk. Deer. A fox.

"Don't worry. Books, paper, crayons. We're set." Sunshine held up a tote bag, then almost laughed at the relief passing through Grady's eyes.

"Well, then, let's take a look at the plans, shall we?"

With Tessa rummaging through the tote, Sunshine joined him at the table, suddenly aware of his height, solid build and a subtle scent of woodsy aftershave. He tugged one of the large blueprint sheets forward. "What we have here is an elevation of the front of the building. As you can see, it looks like any other shop you'd expect to encounter in Hunter Ridge."

It did, and the tension she'd harbored since Saturday eased slightly. The two-story stone structure remained true to the 1940s era in which it had been built. But it was the color rendering of the building on a laptop screen that brought its charm alive. Even with the shop's name lettered on the window, if she didn't know better, she'd think you were entering nothing more controversial than a gift shop or bakery.

"So what do you think?"

It would be nothing but stubbornness that kept her from admitting its acceptability. She raised her eyes to his, startled by the intent scrutiny of his gaze. "It appears tastefully done."

He gave a brisk, satisfied nod and tapped a key on the laptop to bring up another rendering. "The second floor is reserved for an office and stock, but this is the front interior. As you can see, it gives the impression of what you'd expect of an old-fashioned hardware store."

Lots of wood. Retention of the beamed ceiling and polished wood flooring. Indirect lighting.

"And this—" his gaze, now uncertain, remained on her as he moved to the next screen "—is the interior rear of the building."

The game processing area. But it looked as modern and benign as any restaurant kitchen with its massive stainless-steel island, vertical freezers and oversize sinks. The heavy double doors, of course, led to a graveled parking lot out back. The comings and goings of hunters and their game would be discreetly conducted away from the public eye.

"So can the Co-op live with this?"

Did it matter? He'd plainly told her it was there to stay. That the Co-op had only itself to blame if its neighbor was less than ideal for the next three years.

She stepped back from the table and farther from the imposing presence of Grady. "I can't speak for the other members of the Co-op, but I see nothing objectionable here. As you indicated, it's low profile. Nothing blatantly offensive to the sensibilities of others."

"I'm glad you agree."

She offered a coaxing smile. "Would you have any objections if I took printouts of the color designs to the Artists' Co-op meeting tomorrow night?"

He studied her for a long moment, as if hesitant to turn loose the illustrations. "Maybe I should speak with them personally. Deal with their concerns. I can rearrange my schedule."

Grady Hunter in attendance? Not a good idea.

"Thank you, but as the saying goes, a picture paints a thousand words." She didn't want the more contentious members haranguing Grady if he were there in person.

Unquestionably, the growing artists' community needed to be fairly represented in local government and she'd committed to being their voice. But they didn't need to further turn the longtime residents of Hunter Ridge against them with unreasonable demands. "I'll take responsibility for the prints and won't allow anyone to photograph or otherwise copy them."

"I have your word on that?" A half smile surfaced, as if recognizing his wasn't a trusting nature any more than hers was.

"You do. And I'll return the printouts as soon as possible." It was a good excuse to come back to Hunter's Hideaway. Maybe she could take a closer look at the old photographs in the hallway—and the ones in his office, as well.

He studied her a moment longer, as though trying to convince himself of her trustworthiness, and her face warmed under his scrutiny. Then abruptly he reached over to the laptop to press the print key for each of the illustrations he'd shown her. Straightening again, he gave her a challenging look. "Since I have your word..."

He moved to stand over a credenza, where a printer whirred its output, then removed the pages from the tray. Frowning, he held them aloft. "Looks as though it needs a new black ink cartridge. I'll be back in a minute."

As he headed into the hallway, she confirmed Tessa was occupied, then approached a grouping of framed photographs that had caught her eye. Were the faces of her ancestors captured here? If only she had time to scrutinize them. If only...

She darted a look toward the door and, before she could stop herself, she whipped out her cell phone from her jacket pocket.

But as she raised it, zoomed in on one of the old photos, she paused. She'd given her word not to copy the building illustrations, the implication clear that she'd not use them in any way against Grady's family. Would capturing the old photographs in an attempt to find something that she *could* use against the Hunters be breaking that vow?

A muscle in her throat tightened.

Grady would be back any moment. Yes, as he'd pointed out, the photos might not have any connection to his family. But who knew when she'd again have an opportunity to examine evidence that might provide substance to her grandmother's tale?

It was now or never.

Aligning the camera lens once more, she glanced toward her daughter concentrating on the coloring book in her lap. Her daughter in whom she intended to instill the hallmarks of good character, determined that she wouldn't follow in her father's footsteps.

With a soft sigh and a lingering look at the photos, she pocketed her phone—just as Grady strode back into the room.

"How did it go?" Grandma Jo's voice came from behind him where he stood on the front porch, watching as Sunshine's SUV backed out of a parking spot.

Cutting off his apprehensive thoughts, Grady responded. "She agreed that the store design is, in her words, 'tastefully done.' So I don't think Mom will get pushback from her during the election."

"Excellent. Well done, Grady."

His heart swelled at the praise, something Grandma Jo didn't lavish unless merited. Sunshine had been cooperative, but what about the other Co-op members who'd view the renderings? He should have insisted that if the printouts went to the meeting, he be part of the package, too. But those dark, appealing eyes, the soft coaxing voice, had won him over.

Hadn't he learned his lesson six years ago?

"Ms. Carston doesn't stand a chance against your mother." Grandma's tone brooked no argument. "While the artists she represents will rally, there aren't enough to swing a vote."

"Garrett says she's not concentrating exclusively on the artist community." His pastor cousin was often privy to behind-the-scenes rumblings—aka gossip. "She's digging deep to learn what others might like to see change in Hunter Ridge and promising to represent their viewpoint, as well."

"I'm not concerned." Grandma Jo's chin lifted. "We've had Hunters on the town council since its beginnings."

"True." Aunts, uncles, cousins. One day, if he couldn't run fast enough, he'd probably get lassoed into the role, too. But hopefully that was a long way off—if ever. He had too many other things he hoped to accomplish and no taste for politics.

"Again, Grady, good job." Grandma Jo patted his arm. "We can always count on you."

She returned inside and he restlessly stepped off the porch. Grandma was a straight shooter who wasn't afraid to look you in the eye and give you her honest opinion. He'd gotten a no-holds-barred appraisal from her six years ago. She was giving him her equally honest opinion now.

She trusted him.

But, as she'd reminded him that long ago day when things had fallen apart with Jasmine, a reputation once shattered might be patched together—but people would forever be on the lookout for cracks.

There would be no cracks on his watch.

Nevertheless, why hadn't he confessed to Grandma Jo that he'd sent Sunshine off into the world with photocopies of their latest business endeavor?

Chapter Three

"Things could have been worse," Sunshine admitted to Tori as she closed the apartment door behind her Wednesday night. "Nobody stoned me, although I did see Gideon eyeing a molded concrete owl used as a doorstop in the public library's conference room."

More than once, though, she'd wished for the calming presence of Co-op member Benton Mason, her loyal supporter on about any stance she took. But he was working at his part-time maintenance job at Hunter's Hideaway tonight.

Tori set aside the book she'd been reading, her gaze sympathetic. "How was the turnout?"

"Good. About seventeen. Eighteen, maybe." She moved into the open area that served as a dining/living room to put a folder of meeting notes and Grady's printouts on a flat-topped trunk. Then she dropped into a chair opposite where Tori was seated on the sofa and proceeded to rummage through her fringed leather purse. "You haven't seen a sparkly turquoise pen wandering around here have you? I went to pull it out tonight and it was gone."

"No. That's the one your father gave you for high school graduation, isn't it?"

"Yeah." Graduation had been one of the few milestones in her life that Gordon Haynes had remembered to acknowledge. Her wedding and the birth of Tessa had escaped his radar. She sighed and set aside her purse, determined to look for the sentimental item later. Then she glanced at the closed door leading to Tessa's bedroom. "Did you have any trouble getting her to bed?"

"Not too much, although at first she insisted on waiting for you to get home. She wanted to make sure you didn't get locked out. I told her I'd make sure."

"I don't know what's made her so anxious these past few weeks. It started shortly before school started."

"Even kindergarten can be demanding. Schools expect a lot out of kids these days."

"I suppose. But at least this district seems to focus on the basics, on getting the kids grounded academically. I guess we'll wait and see how many times she comes to get me tonight." With a sigh, Sunshine scooted forward to adjust a throw pillow behind her back, then settled in once again.

"Thanks again, Tori, for helping out with her. With the gallery and all the behind-the-scenes business that goes with it, I haven't had as much time as I'd like to meet with potential voters outside the arts community. You know, to find out what their vision is for Hunter Ridge. Although I might edge out Irvin Baydlin, I know the likelihood of beating Elaine Hunter is slim. But I don't stand a chance with either of them if I can't convince others that I can adequately represent them, too."

"I'm more than happy to be here. With things up in the air between Heath and me…" She gazed down at the diamond engagement ring on her left hand.

"He'll come around."

But for reasons that weren't yet clear, Tori's fiancé had

decided they needed space. So at Sunshine's invitation, she'd loaded her car with clothes and the tools of her artistic trade and come to Hunter Ridge.

"I appreciate, too, that you're willing to help me with family research while you're here. I haven't had any free time to explore the truth of anything I remember Grandma saying. Honestly, I don't know where to start."

With little time to call her own, she hadn't so much as confirmed that her great-great-grandparents had been in this region at the same time as the Hunters whose descendants now called this area home. She had no idea if "the ridge of the hunter" her Apache great-great-grandmother had purportedly referred to was truly a reference to Hunter Ridge—or just a coincidence.

Tori drew in a breath, her expression doubtful. "About that research, Sunshine. I'm not sure that—"

Her words were halted by a knock at the door that led to small studios, storage space, a fire escape and stairs to the gallery below.

"Hold that thought, Tori. I think Candy's here to let me know she's locking up for the night." The gallery hours were ten to six, but two nights a week—Wednesday and Saturday, mid-May through mid-September—they remained open until nine. Candy had covered for her while Sunshine met with the Co-op members.

"Hey, Sunshine." Ever perky, the early-twenties brunette standing in the hall was nevertheless smiling more than usual. "Sorry to interrupt, but there's a man downstairs who'd like to speak with you."

"Does he have a name?"

Her fair cheeks flushed and she lowered her voice. "He didn't say and I forgot to ask. I guess I got flustered. He's one of those ruggedly handsome types with dreamy eyes, a yummy voice and a killer smile."

The description fit blond-haired, blue-eyed Sawyer Banks, owner of the Echo Ridge Outpost down the street. Sunshine had run into him at the grocery store that day and they'd chatted a few minutes. But as a newcomer to town, Candy hadn't yet met many of the locals and certainly not one who didn't hang out with the artsy set. But Sawyer was hardly the type to come calling to borrow a cup of sugar, so he must have something else on his mind.

"I'll be right back, Tori." She followed Candy down the stairs.

At the bottom of the steps, she didn't immediately see him as her gaze swept the open space, its hardwood floors glinting under soft, strategically placed lighting. Breathing in the faint, familiar scent of oil paints and leather, she noted with satisfaction the pleasing arrangement of the Co-op's offerings. Oils, watercolors and acrylics. Pottery. Ceramic tiles. Leather handbags. Jewelry. Embroidered pillows and clothing. As the daughter of artists, albeit one of them a mostly absentee father, Sunshine felt right at home.

Candy having hurried on her way home through the front door, Sunshine called out to the seemingly empty space, "Hello?"

"Over here," a low male voice returned and, as she looked toward the rear of the gallery, her heart lurched.

Not Sawyer. Grady Hunter.

Dressed in jeans, work boots and a gray long-sleeved chamois shirt, the big man looked out of place surrounded by clear glass shelving and spotlighted by canister lights. Or was it that the gallery appeared incompatible in the presence of the broad-shouldered, dark-haired man?

"What brings you here this evening, Mr. Hunter?" Surely he hadn't expected her to drive out to his place tonight to return the printouts immediately after the meeting? But she'd have to turn them over to him now—so there'd be no follow-up visit to the hallowed halls of Hunter's Hideaway. She should have snapped a picture of those old photos on his walls when she'd had a chance.

His expression intent, Grady gently placed a delicate piece of hand-blown glass back on the shelf in front of him. Then he looked up at her with a proud smile, as if relieved that his big hands had successfully accomplished the feat.

"It's Grady, Sunshine. Remember?"

His blue eyes skimmed appreciatively over her as he approached and, to her irritation, her heart beat faster. Oh, yes, he was as engaging as the rumors had suggested. That disarming grin and unexpected cooperative spirit at their last two meetings had caught her off guard. But she was ready for him tonight. Armor in place.

Nevertheless, she offered a smile, finding it difficult to suppress. But she'd make him ask her for the printouts, if only to see what excuse he'd make for coming to collect them. "How may I help you…Grady?"

He nodded toward the north wall of the gallery. "I'm giving you a heads-up that there will be increased activity next door for the next couple of days."

He couldn't have phoned the gallery and left a message? "Activity, as in noise?"

"Bingo. I've discussed it with Ted and we think we can work things out to meet our deadline with only weekday disturbance."

"Thank you." Cooperative *and* considerate. And although Candy was right—he did have dreamy eyes and a yummy voice—she couldn't let that distract her.

"So…" He tilted his head. "How did the meeting go tonight?"

Uneasy about that, was he? He didn't *look* uneasy,

though. In fact, as usual, he appeared as relaxed and self-assured as she'd expect a privileged Hunter to be. But hadn't there been a fleeting uncertainty in his eyes when he'd turned over the printouts to her yesterday?

"I can't say there was celebrating in the streets, but the drawings you provided set the minds of the majority at rest. At least for now."

"Glad to hear it." But a crease formed on his forehead. "No concerns I need to be made aware of?"

How much should she tell him? Certainly not the details of a sometimes heated discussion. As expected, Gideon had pointed out that they wouldn't be stuck in this position if *she* hadn't negotiated the lease renewal for three years. Also, that by now advising them not to take any action at this point, she was cozying up to the opposition in the upcoming election. But, fortunately, most members saw the reasonableness of her counsel.

She moved away to straighten a sculpture on its pedestal, then glanced at Grady. "There were some concerns, yes. That occasional game processing taking place right next door might be off-putting to the clientele the gallery is attempting to attract. A few members were, shall we say, disturbed. There was…talk of a petition."

A petition? "It's a little late for that, don't you think? Unless you plan to use this issue to boost your standing at the polls."

Color tinged her cheeks. "I didn't say it was my idea."

"Everything was done aboveboard, out in the open. I don't know who told you that space was to be a bookstore. Maybe it was someone's idea of a joke?"

Or the doing of his aunt Charlotte, who owned the gallery space. She and her big-city lawyers not only grabbed custody of her toddler son, but just about cleaned out

Uncle Doug. That was what rallied the family to pull together and form Hunter Enterprises as a future protective measure.

"We've had this plan for the game supply store in the works," he continued, "and preliminary approvals acquired long before the Co-op leased the property next door to it."

"I understand that and I did make that point to everyone at the meeting."

This kind of thing was exactly what Mom didn't need—misinformed people starting up a petition that she'd have to address in her campaign. But that was the least of her and Dad's worries right now. Despite the family's urging, with Luke's wedding scheduled for last weekend she'd postponed surgery until today. In fact, he'd just come back from the regional medical center in Show Low.

With effort, he drew his thoughts back to the present. "You said earlier that the Co-op signed a three-year lease, right? If Co-op members are so bent out of shape, why don't they simply sublet this place, find a new spot and be done with it? There are plenty of available properties."

In fact, Hunter Enterprises had bought several—like the one where the game supply store would go—to keep longtime friends from going bankrupt. But others were now bank owned or the absentee owners continued to fork over the mortgage payment until an upswing in the economy allowed them to unload the property.

Sunshine brushed back her hair. "Unfortunately, there's a nonsublease stipulation in the contract."

That figured. Aunt Char wouldn't risk a Hunter subletting one of the prizes she'd managed to wrest from them.

"Look," she continued. "I was quite firm that a petition would cause hard feelings in the community toward us—the 'aliens.' You *have* heard us called that, haven't you?"

A glint of amusement now lit her eyes.

"Aliens. Outsiders." His own smile tugged. "Just as I've heard those of us who've long made this our home labeled 'old-timers'."

"So you can see it's not to our benefit to further antagonize the community. Or at least that's my standpoint."

"Spoken with the finesse of a true politician."

"I'm not a politician. I'm merely someone who feels passionate about the arts and fair play."

"Fair play? Pushing into a community uninvited and trying to extinguish the core character of a town?" Newcomers needed to accept Hunter Ridge for what it was or move on. Even a newcomer who looked mighty attractive tonight in denim capris, sandals and an off-the-shoulder embroidered tunic.

"Look, Grady—"

"Mommy?" A plaintive voice called from the top of the staircase and a barefooted, pajama-clad Tessa eased down one step at a time. "I think there's something in my closet."

Grady caught the distress in Sunshine's eyes.

"Sweetie, there's nothing in your closet but your clothes."

"But there *is*." The girl's eyes widened as she spied him, and then she crouched down on the step.

Sunshine sent a look of apology in his direction. "Give me a few minutes to get her back to bed."

"Sure. And about those building renderings I gave you…"

"I'll drop them off tomorrow after I've looked at them again, if that's okay?"

"That won't be necessary. Shredding them would be fine."

Sunshine frowned.

"There you are, Tessa." A feminine voice called from the top of the staircase and a short-haired young blonde appeared, relief tingeing her tone when she spied the little girl. "I'm sorry, Sunshine. I stepped into the bathroom for a minute or two."

"It's okay, Tori. Don't worry about it."

The other woman took Tessa's hand, her gaze touching on him curiously. Sunshine caught the look.

"Tori, I'd like you to meet Grady Hunter. Grady, this is my friend Tori Janner. She's visiting from Jerome."

"Hunter?" The name was spoken almost cautiously.

"As in our soon-to-be next-door neighbor," Sunshine supplied. "He stopped by to let us know to expect more activity tomorrow."

"I'll get out my earplugs." She tugged lightly on Tessa's hand and the two returned upstairs.

Grady shifted. "I'd better let you go trounce whatever is in Tessa's closet. Monsters?"

Sunshine gave a weary sigh. "Monsters I could deal with. Moms are natural-born slayers of monsters. This, unfortunately, is a more vague anxiety that's had her upset since shortly before school started."

"Once she makes friends and settles into a new environment, those worries will evaporate."

"That's my hope." But she didn't sound as if she believed his words.

He moved closer to look down on her with mock chastisement. "Now, don't *you* go worrying about Tessa's worrying. You know what the Good Book says about that."

Or maybe she didn't know. She'd only recently started attending Christ's Church of Hunter Ridge. Was that a politically motivated move? He'd like to think a single mom had more concern for her child's spiritual welfare than that. But God gave people more freedom of choice than he would if running the show himself.

With a sigh, she stared down at the floor and his chest tightened. This kid thing must be getting to her.

"It's just that…" She shook her head, lost in thought.

Without thinking, he reached out and gently lifted her chin with his fingertips, her startled eyes meeting his.

"Stop with the worrying, Sunshine."

She froze, staring up at him as the warmth of his fingers shot a bolt of awareness through her. An unsettling, although not unpleasant feeling. But this was Grady Hunter. A male cut from the same bolt of cloth as her ex.

She stepped back to break the connection, fearful he'd feel the pounding of her heart. "Believe me, I'm doing my best *not* to."

"Well, good, then."

Their eyes remained locked for an uncomfortable moment, and then she glanced to the top of the staircase. "Are you sure you don't want me to drop off the design printouts tomorrow?"

"Like I said, destroy them."

There went her excuse to visit Hunter's Hideaway again.

He moved toward the door, then paused in front of a watercolor painting displayed on an easel. "I noticed that several of these bear the intertwined initials ESC. Is that you?"

The subject of this painting in particular could have clued him in on the identity of the artist, as well. The child, in partial shadow and facing slightly away, might easily be recognizable as Tessa to someone who knew her. Reluctantly, Sunshine joined him where he continued to study the painting.

"The *E* stands for Elizabeth. Sunshine's always been the name I go by." Her father, who'd been around more often in those early years, had bestowed it on her when she was a toddler.

"You're extremely talented."

"Thank you."

"This is for sale?" His brow furrowed as his gaze met hers uncertainly. "A painting of your daughter?"

He sounded almost disapproving.

"It's not a portrait." With effort, she suppressed the defensiveness his words provoked. "It could be any little girl with a Native American patterned blanket clutched in her arms. Customers like that Southwestern touch."

"It's very striking."

"Thanks."

He moved to the door and she followed to lock up.

"You *will* keep me informed, won't you?" He paused in the doorway, all business now. "I mean, if there are any developments with the Co-op members I should be made aware of? I'm available to meet with them, to answer questions and set things straight."

"As I said earlier, I believe the proposed petition has been squelched." At least Gideon had backed off for the time being.

Grady looked as if he wanted to say something more but instead nodded a goodbye. She locked up and dimmed the lights. Then wearily heading up the stairs, two troubling thoughts remained foremost.

Why did Grady touching her take her breath away?

And please, Lord, don't let me be present if Grady Hunter and Gideon Edlow ever cross paths.

Chapter Four

Whoever would have thought when Grady insisted she destroy the printouts rather than returning them that another excuse to visit Hunter's Hideaway would be delivered to her doorstep so speedily?

Now, Thursday afternoon, trailing his younger sister Rio down the hallway to his office, she could hardly believe her good fortune. There was an added bonus, as well. Rio said Grady had stepped out and hadn't yet returned. So if she could manage to ditch Rio, she might not only find her missing pen, but have an opportunity for another look at the photographs on Grady's wall. On closer examination, would a face in one of them stand out as resembling her mother or grandmother?

"This is the only place I think I could have lost it," Sunshine said as Rio flipped on the light and they stepped into Grady's office. "I used it to jot down notes when I was waiting in the lobby the other day, then distinctly remember putting it back into my jacket pocket. That's the last time I saw it. At Hunter's Hideaway. And since it wasn't in your lost and found, hopefully it's in here somewhere. It was a gift from my father, so it's special."

After having thoroughly combed her apartment, SUV,

tote bag and jacket pockets that morning, it had taken mental backtracking to figure out the possible whereabouts of the pen. That maybe when she'd pulled out her phone here a few days ago, she'd accidentally dislodged the pen. It was a long shot, but if it had dropped to the thick, patterned area rug, she wouldn't have heard it hit the floor. Engrossed in her coloring book, Tessa might not have noticed, either.

Rio adjusted the wooden louvered blinds to admit more natural light. "Let's take a look."

Ignoring a prick of disappointment that Grady's sister chose not to return immediately to the front desk, Sunshine gave a longing look at the photographs on the wall, then embarked on the quest for her pen.

"I sat in this area with Tessa for a few minutes," she explained, leaning over to check under the chairs and lamp-topped table, "then stood over there with Grady to look at the blueprints and his laptop screen."

She wouldn't mention wandering the perimeters of the room with a camera in her hand.

"If it's here, we'll find it."

"Thanks, but I hate taking you away from your work." *Maybe you'd better get back to it. Hint. Hint.*

"Maybe Grady found it." Rio optimistically checked out the pencil cup on the desk, then shook her head and they resumed the search.

"Aah, here it is." As tempting as it was to nudge the colorful pen farther under the edge of the rug with her toe, Sunshine reluctantly bent to retrieve it. So much for thinking God had rewarded her with an opportunity to explore. "Ta-da!"

"What's going on?" Grady's deep voice drew her attention as he crossed the threshold of his office, surprise at seeing her there evident in his eyes.

"Sunshine was looking for the pen she lost here the other day." Rio cast her a bright smile. "Her dad had given it to her."

"I hadn't realized you'd lost something or I could have looked around for you."

"No problem."

When Rio disappeared into the hallway, Grady moved to his desk and placed his laptop case on the oak surface. "You're close to your dad, are you?"

Clutching the pen in her hand, she moved to stand across the desk from him. "Not exactly."

A puzzled look shadowed his eyes.

"I don't mean to sound mysterious," she amended. "It's just that, well, I never saw a lot of him. He wasn't around much—he never got around to marrying my mom."

Grady's expression filled with sympathy. "Rough."

"But I'm over it." She slipped the pen into her purse, careful to push it securely to the bottom. "So I guess it's corny to get overly sentimental about a high school graduation gift."

"Not corny at all. I'm glad you found it."

His reassuring words comforted. Made her feel less silly for clinging to the pen for all these years. "Like I said, it isn't that he's an intentionally bad father or anything like that. He has a busy career, and has always traveled frequently."

"What did he do for a living that took him away so often?"

She trailed her fingers along the edge of the desk, remembering as a child how excited she'd be when he put in an appearance—and how disappointed when he left without a goodbye. "He's an artist. Jewelry maker. His work is featured in shops and galleries throughout the Southwest."

"Wow. So that's where you got your talent."

"And from my mother. And her mother and her mother's mother before that. I've heard stories that my great-great-grandmother had strong creative leanings, as well."

"That's quite a lineage. You should be proud of that."

"Oh, I am." Why was she telling him this? Searching for a change in topic, she glanced at one of the wildlife photographs on the wall. "Who's the photographer?"

He looked up from where he was booting up his laptop. "What's that?"

"Who took these amazing wildlife shots? I noticed them the last time I was here. I'd love to get a print of this deer for my living room."

"That can be arranged."

"You know the artist? Whoever took these has an incredible eye for detail. A great understanding of composition."

"I'll pass on the compliment."

"Is he local? Or she, I guess I should say. A focus on wildlife isn't the sole domain of males."

"He's about as local as you can get." Grady grinned sheepishly and suddenly she got it.

"You took these pictures?" She moved closer to the one of the fox. "They're amazing. I didn't know you were a professional photographer."

He came around the desk to stand by her. "Define *professional.*"

"Talented. Gifted. And receiving payment for your work."

"Then, I guess I don't qualify."

She stared at him. "You're kidding. Why not?"

"Just a hobby."

"You mean you've never tried to sell anything?"

He folded his arms. "Wildlife photographers are a

dime a dozen—especially with the advent of digital cameras. Go online and type in *wildlife photography* and see the results you get. There are bunches of talented people out there."

"And you're one of them."

He looked shyly pleased at her words, but she could only stare at him in surprise. "Has no one ever told you how accomplished you are? How sensitively you've captured the nuances of nature? It's criminal that you're not being paid to do this. I could—"

No, while she could easily prove her point that his work could garner sales, she wouldn't offer to take his photos to the gallery. Not only would some of the other Co-op members—like Gideon—frown on that, but why should she, a struggling artist herself, smooth the rocky road for a Hunter?

Drawn to the charismatic outdoorsman with an artistic eye, how quickly she'd forgotten he was where *he* was today and she was where *she* was because his ancestor had cheated hers.

"Photography is a private thing for me." Grady turned his full attention to the petite woman standing beside him, absorbing her evaluation of his work. He'd never talked to anyone outside the family about his photography. And seldom with family, although if he was going to get his plans off the ground to add a photographic element to the Hunter Ridge lineup, that would soon be changing. "Don't you find that yourself? That in each of your creations you've poured a piece of yourself into it and find it hard to release it into the hands of others?"

He still didn't understand how she could put that extraordinary watercolor of Tessa up for sale. To offer it to some stranger to hang on the wall of their home or office just because they forked over a credit card.

With a soft laugh, she cast him a wary look, no doubt recognizing where his thoughts were going. "A similar reluctance may have been the case for me years ago but now, with a child to support, the almighty dollar wins out every time. I definitely agree with you, though. Each creation carries the creator's fingerprint, so to speak."

He nodded. Although she'd pushed herself beyond the self-conscious unwillingness to expose her work to the criticism of others—the thing that held him back— she nevertheless understood his hesitance to go public.

Sunshine pointed at the photo of a fox he'd taken last winter. "Like this one. I don't imagine you conveniently shot it through your kitchen window, did you? While it's a moment caught in time, it's my guess you observed the comings and goings of this elusive creature, studied the angle of the sun, glare off the snow, and gave thought to composition. You knew the mood and message you wanted to convey before the shutter clicked. All three of these photos strongly reflect the artist behind the lens."

Artist. He didn't much care for that label. He thought of himself as more of an observer of wildlife who'd learned the tricks of capturing an image. One who made use of a camera's technical features to produce a pleasing photo.

They talked for some time about his current preference for black-and-white, use of focal length and the considerations made in composition. About the challenges of wildlife. It was in many ways oddly affirming to speak with someone knowledgeable about those aspects of his work.

"Oh, my goodness." Sunshine cringed as she looked at the clock on his credenza. "I barged in on your day to look for my pen, but didn't intend to take up all your time."

He smiled at her flustered movements, the appealing flush on her face. "I didn't have anything scheduled for the rest of the afternoon. I enjoyed our visit."

"I did, too." Another wave of color rose in her cheeks. Then she abruptly turned away. "But I need to get back to the gallery."

Halfway to the door, she glanced at the grouping of vintage photos on the wall and paused. "So are these more of your mother's yard-sale finds?"

Curiously relieved that she hadn't dashed off, he moved to stand beside her. "Not these. I latched on to them when my grandpa Hunter passed away when I was nineteen."

"So this is your family?"

"Some are." He studied the photos, then pointed to a stiffly composed group of people standing outside a cabin. "Like this one."

"Do you know who they are?"

"These two are my great-great-grandparents. Harrison—he went by Duke—and Pearl Hunter. They came here on the cusp of the twentieth century. Acquired land in the very early 1900s. The youngster hanging on to the mangy-looking dog is my great-grandfather, Carson. And his sisters are next to him."

"And what about these two?" Sunshine touched her finger lightly to the nonreflective glass, noting another man and a woman off to the side. "If I'm not mistaken, the woman looks to be Native American."

A muscle twitched in his jaw. "Those people lived on the property. Friends of the family."

That was, if you could call a man who'd betrayed you a friend. Grady had intentionally placed this photo front

and center in his office after Jasmine's underhanded-
ness. A reminder that, as also in the case of Aunt Char's
disloyalty, Hunters had to look out for Hunters first and
foremost. Outsiders couldn't be trusted.

"Do they have names?"

"Walter Royce and his wife, Flora." Their monikers
were emblazoned on his brain. "And yes, she's Native
American. White Mountain Apache."

Sunshine stepped closer, her gaze more intent. Like his
mom, she seemed enthralled with old-time photographs
and the stories they held.

"That woven blanket draped over her arm… It's such
an interesting pattern. One I'd like to incorporate in one
of my paintings." She looked to him hopefully. "Would
you mind if I took a picture of it?"

He shrugged. "Have at it."

She eagerly slipped her cell phone from her purse and
snapped a few shots. "Inspiration sometimes comes from
directions you least expect, doesn't it?"

"I guess so." Actually, he *knew* so. How many times
had his eyes been drawn to something because of the texture, the shadow, the sheer beauty of it and his fingers
itched to reach for his camera? Like right now. With Sunshine's dark eyes bright with excitement and natural light
from the windows glinting off her glossy black hair and
highlighting a soft cheek and the gentle curve of her lips.

"When do you think this photo was taken?"

"Judging from my great-grandfather's age here, I'm
guessing about 1906, 1907, maybe?"

A wistful look flickered in her eyes. "It must be wonderful to trace your family back this far. To know that
these pine trees on the property shaded them as they do
your family now. That every single day you're walking
where they walked."

"Yeah, I guess it is remarkable." Her enthusiasm was almost contagious, and he found himself smiling. "In fact, the original cabin in this picture and the one the Royces lived in are still on the property."

Her eyes widened. "You're kidding. I'd love to see them sometime."

While they weren't rotting or anything like that—his family had seen to it that they were well maintained— they hadn't been modernized. "They're nothing fancy, you understand."

"I wouldn't expect them to be. But I'd love to see buildings that hold such history."

"Well, then, sometime when you don't have to rush off, I can arrange that."

From the indecisive flicker in her eyes, for a moment he thought she might claim that getting back to the gallery was of minor importance and insist that now was as good a time as any for a tour. But when she merely uttered a thank-you, he determined the perceived wavering on her part must have been in his imagination.

Wishful thinking?

Unfortunately, that could only get him into trouble. He'd heard grumblings at a family breakfast meeting that morning about Sunshine's earlier visit to the Hideaway. Uncle Doug warned that she might be snooping around for something to use against Grady's mother in the upcoming election—although neither he nor Uncle "Mac" McCrae could come up with exactly what that might be. Aunt Suzy—Dad's sister and Uncle Mac's wife— reiterated that until more was known about her sister-in-law's health status, everyone should keep silent about it with those outside the family. As political opponents, Sunshine Carston and Irvin Baydlin didn't need to be alerted just yet.

Grandma Jo, fortunately, had put in a good word as to his "proactive" endeavors to soothe the ruffled feathers of the Artists' Co-op members regarding the new Hunter business. But how would he explain escorting Sunshine around the property to see old family cabins?

"Grady?" Sunshine's curious eyes met his, no doubt wondering where he'd mentally wandered off.

"Let me know when you're available to take a look at the cabins, and I'll check my schedule." Maybe he could put her off for a while. With all there was to do at the Hideaway with the influx of hunters and with details of the new wild game supply store demanding his attention, he'd have an excuse to beg off if he needed one.

She moved to the door, then paused, a thoughtful look on her face. "Your mother wouldn't happen to be around this afternoon, would she? I wanted to ask her about—"

"No, I'm afraid not. She's out of town this week."

"Oh? I'll get in touch with her later, then."

As Sunshine disappeared into the hallway, Grady again studied the old photograph of the original Hunter's Hideaway. Remembered the deceit that had severed a friendship.

Was Sunshine's request to talk to his mother an innocent one? Or had she somehow gotten wind of her opponent's possible Achilles' heel and today's visit was nothing more than a fishing expedition to learn more?

Chapter Five

"I think I *may* have confirmed it, Tori." Sunshine glanced at her friend Saturday morning. "Not only is 'the ridge of the hunter' likely the same as Hunter Ridge, but I may now have proof that my ancestors knew the Hunter family just as in the family legend."

With satisfaction, she tapped the screen of her laptop computer, where she'd uploaded photos from her phone. They were the first images she'd ever seen of her legendary ancestors if, indeed, these two were her great-great-grandparents. When Grady pointed them out, named names she'd never before heard, it was all she could do not to topple over in amazement as the pieces fit together.

"A pioneer family named Hunter, can you believe it? Who not only lived in the area that one day would neighbor Hunter Ridge, but who were friends of another couple—an Anglo husband with an Apache wife. Identical to the family story related by my grandma."

Had Grady noticed her excitement?

"You said her name was Flora?" Tori inspected one of the photos. "That doesn't sound like an Indian name, but she does look like the full-blooded White Mountain Apache of family folklore, doesn't she? I can see where your jet-black hair, dark eyes and beautiful warm complexion could have been inherited from her. Do you see any other family resemblance to either of them?"

"Flora's build and facial structure is similar to my grandmother's—Flora's granddaughter—if indeed this is my ancestor. And Walter?" Sunshine frowned. "I'm not sure."

"This is wild." Tori stepped back, but her attention remained fixed on the screen. "I have to admit, I didn't think there was any substance to those tall tales you told me."

"Well, we don't know for sure." But something deep inside Sunshine bubbled up, telling her she was looking into the faces of those who'd come before her. "I never knew their names. But it's not as if I've had some pristine lineage traced back to the *Mayflower*, you know. The family on Mom's side has been fragmented. There was never an interest in documenting our ancestry. Grandma's mother died when Grandma was a teen. That's who she'd have gotten her information from, and Grandma's grandma died before that. So even though my great-grandma knew her parents' names, that wouldn't necessarily have been passed down to her own daughter."

"Gets complicated, doesn't it? I didn't even know my own great-grandparents' names until I did research."

"It's not as if my grandmother tried to verify any of this, either. I mean, the substance of the story she passed down was focused solely on the unfortunate fact that our ancestors were cheated out of property by someone they considered a friend."

Tori crossed the room to lower herself onto the sofa. "Even if these two are related to you, that doesn't mean there's any truth to the core of that story. You know, that Hunters grabbed their land or anything."

"No, but…" Stories had to start somewhere, didn't they?

"So what's next?"

Sunshine moved to a front window overlooking the road through town, then pushed aside a sheer curtain to watch the activity below. "Well, I guess I need to go online and see if those names can be verified on one of those genealogy websites."

"You know it isn't as easy as those TV shows depict, don't you? I mean, they have professional genealogists who do months of background research. Then when the celebrity shows up with cameras rolling, they tap a few keys and pull up the proof as if they'd just discovered it."

"I know, but it's somewhere to start. I'll begin with what I know about Mom and Grandma and work my way back."

"People in the olden days didn't always have birth certificates. And your Apache ancestor likely didn't."

"True." Sunshine rested her forehead on the cool pane of glass, trying to better see what was going on below. Was that Grady Hunter hauling a box out of a navy blue SUV in front of the building next door?

"What are you looking at?"

"Oh, nothing." Sunshine moved away from the window and sat down. "So has my family mystery intrigued you enough that you're willing to help me? I know you have reservations about how the story involves the Hunters."

"That's the part that I'm most concerned about. But I've researched my own family and found it rewarding. So I'd be happy to do that for you while you're seeing to the gallery, Co-op business and getting out to meet your future constituency."

"You're the best friend in the world, Tori."

But when would Tori's fiancé recognize the treasure

he had in her? He hadn't asked her to return the engagement ring, so that had to mean there was hope, didn't it?

"It's the least I can do, with you letting me stay here. I couldn't stay in Jerome and risk bumping into Heath every time I turned around. Or having people ask me about him, probing to find out what's going on with us when I don't know myself."

"Have you—" Sunshine paused, knowing this was sensitive territory "—considered breaking the engagement yourself? Provoking him into working through whatever it is that's gotten into him?"

"I know it sounds stupid." Tori looked down at the ring on her hand. "But I'm not ready to close the door yet. I love him."

Ah, yes, love.

Sunshine had been there herself and couldn't point fingers at her friend now. "Whatever happens—wedding or no wedding—know that I'm here for you."

When Tori returned to her room, Sunshine again moved restlessly to the window. Yes, that was Grady down there, now talking with the man she knew to be his contractor.

He'd promised to show her those historic cabins, but they hadn't firmed that up. The likelihood that she'd make new discoveries under those roofs to confirm her grandmother's story was slim, but it would be worth a try.

She glanced down at her watch. She had thirty minutes until she had to unlock the gallery doors for another business day.

"Tessa?" she called, intending to see if she'd like to go on a walk, which would coincidentally lead past the renovation of the store next door.

But then she stopped herself.

That thinking—or rather *not* thinking—was exactly

how she'd gotten tangled up with Tessa's father. And *this* guy was a descendent of Duke Hunter.

Windshield wipers beating a steady rhythm, Grady applied the brakes as he rounded another wet curve on the way back from visiting his mother at the hospital Sunday evening. She'd had an adverse reaction to her medications a few days ago, but seemed to have stabilized and might soon come home. Then would begin the long haul of postsurgery physical therapy and chemotherapy treatments.

Man, he hated to see her go through that. Dad, too. *Please, God, heal Mom. We need her.*

Now, halfway between Canyon Springs and Hunter Ridge, twilight had given over to darkness, and clouds from a late-season monsoon rain hung low. The days were rapidly growing shorter and summer was pretty much over as the nighttime temperatures dropped into the midforties. Elections would soon be upon them. Would Mom stick it out or withdraw from the race?

He lowered the volume of the country tune belting out of the stereo speakers. It was a mournful love song that, for some irritating reason, made him think of Sunshine.

He'd been relieved that after their conversation a few days ago, she'd made no further attempts to visit the Hideaway or to try to see his mother. Nor had she pressed him to show her the old family cabins that appeared to have captured her imagination when he'd mentioned them. So his family's concerns that she had ulterior motives were unfounded.

Although he hadn't forgotten that she did have a reputation for stirring things up—for championing the sometimes extremist views of the local artists—he couldn't see her doing anything underhanded, such as using his mother's illness to undermine her during the weeks preceding the election.

Then again, he'd not been that good of a judge of women in the past, had he?

Rounding another curve, his headlights sliced through the dark, and up ahead he spied the flashing emergency lights of a vehicle pulled off to the side of the road. Nasty night to have car trouble.

He slowed, but he'd no more than gotten up to it when he recognized the older-model, burgundy-colored SUV. He'd taken notice of it the day he'd stood on the Hideaway porch and watched it out of sight. Rusted out near a back wheel well, it also boasted a slightly bent bumper with a Hunter Ridge Artists' Cooperative sticker.

Sunshine.

Braking, he abruptly pulled off the rain slick road, then backed up until the rear bumper of his SUV almost kissed the front of the other vehicle. He couldn't be sure with headlights lancing into his back window, but he thought he'd glimpsed someone in the front driver's seat when he'd passed by.

He pulled up the hood of his windbreaker and climbed out, striding through the rain and glare of headlights to make his way to the driver's side window.

"Grady?" a soft, familiar voice came through the partially rolled-down window.

"You okay?"

"Yeah. It died on me. Like, it ran out of steam."

"How long have you been out here?"

"Maybe half an hour or so. It doesn't seem to be a battery problem, though. The lights are working. I'd have called for assistance, but for some reason I can't get a signal on my cell phone."

"We'll deal with your car later. Why don't you hop on out and I'll give you a ride home."

She shifted to look in the backseat. "Stop crying, sweetheart. There's nothing to be afraid of."

She had Tessa with her?

"This is our friend Grady," she continued. "You remember him? Didn't I tell you God would send someone to help us?"

He couldn't catch the child's response, but he heard another murmured reassurance from her mother before Sunshine faced him again. "I'm sorry. You're getting soaked."

"I won't melt. Let's get you both home. Do you have jackets?"

"Yes, and we'll need to take Tessa's booster seat, too."

"No problem."

In no time at all, he transferred the ladies to his vehicle, secured Sunshine's SUV, then set up reflectors to alert any passing traffic.

At last he climbed inside, his hair now plastered to his head and cold rain trickling down the back of his neck. But he hardly noticed.

"Everybody buckled in? Ready to roll?"

Upon hearing the happy affirmatives, he pulled on to the highway and headed toward Hunter Ridge.

"I can't tell you, Grady—" Sunshine leaned in closer, her voice low, he assumed, to keep Tessa from hearing "—how relieved I was to see you. I had no idea who might have pulled up in front of us."

Like Tessa, she'd been scared.

He cleared his throat. "God was watching out for you."

"He was. Thank you."

Grady gave her a reassuring smile, acutely aware of her grateful eyes on him as the windshield wipers beat a steady rhythm. When she settled back into her seat, drawing her jacket more closely around her, he flipped on the heater.

A weary sigh escaped her lips. "Believe it or not, I got that thing out of the shop right after Labor Day. *Again*. It's costing me a small fortune."

"Fairly old vehicle, isn't it?"

"It was old when I bought it, but it's always been reliable. And the four-wheel drive has come in handy since I moved to town."

"Might be time to start looking for a replacement."

"Fat chance."

"If you'll give me your keys when we get back to town, I'll catch a ride with a tow truck and we'll get your SUV to a repair shop." There were several. He'd find out which one she'd been going to and determine if a switch was in order.

"Thanks. But I hate for you to go back out in this."

"No biggie."

"Mommy?" Tessa's query carried from the backseat.

"Yeah, sweetie?"

"I'm hungry."

"I'll fix you something as soon as we get home."

Grady lowered his voice. "I can stop to pick something up for her."

"Thanks, but that won't be necessary. I think because it gets dark earlier now, she thinks it's later than it actually is. She had a late lunch, and a big one at that. Those church-related gatherings sure know how to put on a potluck."

"So you went to church in Canyon Springs? I didn't see you at Christ's Church this morning." Should he have admitted that? Did it sound like he'd been looking for her?

"No, not Canyon Springs. A church on the White

Mountain Apache reservation." Sunshine held out her hands to the heating vent to warm them. "I've gotten involved there since moving to Hunter Ridge. But with Tessa starting school, I realize she needs to get to bed early on Sunday nights. So this was our last full day there until next summer."

He slowed the vehicle as they approached the turnoff to Hunter Ridge, then headed down a steep, forested descent to the bridge over Hunter Creek. On the other side, the twisting road again led upward to the little community he'd always called home. It could be a mean route to negotiate after a snowfall. Sunshine would definitely need four-wheel drive if she intended to keep living here in the winter months.

By the time he pulled in front of the Hunter Ridge Artists' Cooperative, the rain had slackened to a drizzle. Sunshine helped Tessa from the vehicle, and he snared the booster seat, then met them under the awning, where Sunshine ushered her daughter inside.

"Keys, please." He held out his hand.

"You're sure?"

"Positive."

She disengaged the car key from her key chain and handed it to him. "I don't know what we'd have done without you tonight. I wish there was some way I could repay you."

"No need."

She scowled, obviously not satisfied with his answer. Then her gaze swept the dimly lit gallery, her eyes brightening. "I know! I can display some of your wildlife photos here. As a guest artist. I'll prove to you that your work can be a moneymaker."

He stepped back, shaking his head. "I don't think so."

"Why not?"

Why not? Because he couldn't afford to be labeled as an "artist" in this town. Couldn't afford to have his friends and family snickering behind his back or criticizing him for what might be interpreted as joining the very people in the community that had a candidate running against his mother.

"I'm not ready to go there, but thanks for offering."

Disappointment colored her eyes, but she didn't argue. Merely thanked him again and watched from the doorway as he returned to his vehicle. He called a local towing service, then headed out to meet the guy at his garage.

Sunshine's offer to display his photos had been unexpected. A flattering boost to his ego. Tempting, too, even if the offer had been made out of a sense of indebtedness. Unfortunately, for many reasons it wasn't something he could afford to take her up on. Including the fact he had no desire to discover—in such a public forum—that no one wanted to buy his photographs.

Chapter Six

Thankfully, Grady had turned down her offer to display his wildlife photographs. Sunshine had already nixed the idea earlier, but overwhelmed with gratitude that night, she'd wanted to demonstrate how much she appreciated what he'd done for her and Tessa.

Now, four days later, looking lovingly at her daughter across the breakfast table, that sense of appreciation overflowed. If it hadn't been for Grady, who knows how long they'd have sat out there on the dark, rainy road? Or who else might have pulled over to offer assistance?

"So the problem turned out to be something haywire with the fuel pump?" Tori rose from her chair and started clearing dishes.

"Right." The mechanic at the shop the Hunters had long done business with was able to fix it—and she suspected the bill she'd paid was considerably reduced because of the connection to the prominent local family. "The guy at the garage says I should find a replacement vehicle before winter sets in. As if that's going to happen."

Right about now she could sure use that dreamed-of settlement from the property her great-great-grandparents had lost to the Hunters. *Allegedly* lost, as Tori always reminded. Tessa needed new snow boots, car and health insurance were coming due and annual dental and doctor appointments couldn't be put off much longer. Once she proved her grandma's tale held substance, would the Hunters feel obligated to compensate her?

"You know, you're always welcome," Tori said as she rinsed a plate, "to use my car for as long as I'm here."

"I may have to take you up on that." As Tessa scurried off to her room, Sunshine joined her friend in the kitchen. "But I need to figure out a solution for the long run. Right now money is tight."

"At least that Hunter guy was in the right place at the right time." Tori handed her a plate, which Sunshine placed in the dishwasher. "Does it seem weird to be seeing so much of him lately? You know, since you're running against his mother and want to prove his family cheated yours."

"It's awkward sometimes." She loaded two more plates and a handful of utensils. "At other times I forget about that and we just, you know, talk as if those barriers don't exist."

Which was a danger zone she needed to be on guard against.

"He seems nice. Cute, too." Tori's tone held a probing note.

"Don't get any ideas on my behalf." Sunshine gave her friend a warning look. "He's too much like Jerrel. The easygoing, charming, never-knows-a-stranger type. You've noticed, haven't you, how the single gals flock around him at church on Sunday mornings? Yep, too much like Jerrel."

"Jerrel didn't go to church, though."

"I didn't go, either, remember?"

In fact, she'd never graced the door of a church until

after Tessa had been born and her husband—the lead vocalist in a promising regional country band—had decided a child cramped his style. That was when she'd met Tori—at a storefront church in Jerome shortly after Jerrel filed for divorce.

"So what's on your agenda for today, Sunshine?"

To her relief, Tori didn't pursue further talk of Grady Hunter. "I thought I'd take Tessa to the park for a while before I open the gallery."

"When you get back, I'll pull out my sewing machine, and that should keep us busy for the rest of the morning. Tessa wants to make a tote bag, and since my mother started me on simple things like that when I was her age, I think she can handle it. We'll begin with the safety-first basics."

Quilting was Tori's gift to the world, her artistic contribution. A labor of love. Tessa couldn't have a better teacher.

When they reached the park and Tessa had made a beeline for the swings, Sunshine was glad they'd worn light jackets. Although the sun filtered down through overhanging pine branches, it was still a cool, fallish morning. From somewhere above came the skitter of a squirrel's claws on roughened bark, and a chorus of sparrows chirping a cheerful song.

The park had only a handful of kid-friendly amenities. Swings, a merry-go-round and a trio of slides in varying sizes—of which Tessa had proudly graduated to the middlemost. But the park was treed, spacious and nestled in the heart of Hunter Ridge's business district. It was for this location that last spring she'd requested a permit approval for a series of art-in-the-park events. But she'd been turned down.

Maybe next year, if she was elected to the town council?

"Hey! How is everybody this morning?"

Her heart inexplicably lifting at the sound of the familiar voice, Sunshine turned to see Grady striding toward them with that distinctive masculine gait, his impossibly broad shoulders clad in a windbreaker.

"Grady!" To Sunshine's surprise, her daughter let out a cry of welcome and abandoned the swing to run toward him, her oversize jacket flapping around her.

Tessa loved the variations of the cotton jacket's purple color, so Sunshine had given in and bought it from the sale table at the bargain store. She hadn't intended for Tessa to wear it until she'd grown into it in a few years, but this morning Tessa had spied it in the back of the coat closet and insisted on wearing it.

When Tessa reached Grady, she grabbed his hand and gazed happily up at him. "Now you can see how high I can swing."

He glanced at Sunshine, looking slightly taken aback at Tessa's grip on his hand. "I can do that."

Willingly, he allowed her to pull him forward to stand next to her mother.

"Okay. Now watch." Tessa dashed for the swings.

"I'm watching." A grin lit his face at the little girl's enthusiasm. "Do you need a push?"

She shook her head as she lowered herself onto the seat and grasped the swing chains, proud that she didn't need assistance. In a flash, she had herself moving.

"Wow," he said in an aside to Sunshine. "To have that much energy."

She laughed. "I know."

"Do you think her jacket's big enough?" Humor lit his eyes.

He *would* notice. "Obviously you don't fully comprehend the persuasive abilities of a five-year-old."

He folded his arms and slanted her a look. "I have a fairly good idea. Nieces and nephews, you know."

"Are you watching?" a demanding voice called.

"We're watching!" they yelled in unison, then exchanged a glance and laughed.

The kindergartner was pumping herself higher and higher, a determined look on her little face.

"You're doing great, Tessa!" With Grady's words of encouragement impelling her to pump harder, a triumphant smile widened.

Sunshine's heart swelled with love. And regret. Seeing how her daughter openly craved the attention of Grady acutely reminded her of her own absentee father. The longing for a dad's attention. A male role model. As much as she'd hated having a father who wasn't around, here she was repeating history with her own child. The last thing she'd ever intended to have happen.

"Thank you again, Grady, for the rescue Sunday night."

"You're welcome."

"I—" Sunshine tensed as from across the street she glimpsed Gideon Edlow, who'd paused to stare at her and Grady. He was frowning, as though it was any of his business who she talked to. He'd been cantankerous at last night's Co-op meeting. That wasn't anything new, but it was growing increasingly tiresome. Worrisome, as well. With effort, she refocused her attention on Grady, silently willing Gideon to move on.

"Thanks, too, for getting my SUV to someone who not only knows what he's doing, but didn't request I turn over my firstborn for payment."

He looked pleased. "So you have wheels again?"

"I do. But he's of the same mind as you—that I should find a replacement before winter."

Grady's eyes grew thoughtful. "Do you have today off?"

Why did he want to know that? Surely he didn't intend to go car shopping with her. "No, I have to open the gallery at ten. But we thought we'd get some sunshine while we can. Winter is just around the corner."

"It is."

"But even with summer basically over, I have plenty to do at the Co-op as well as campaign-related things—" She caught his eye apologetically. After all, she was his mother's opponent. "And I have plans to expand the Co-op's offerings. While anyone—as your sister-in-law Delaney has done—can take private lessons with an artist-mentor, I'd like to see classes geared to those in middle and high school."

"Provide them with more hands-on exposure to the arts?"

"Exactly. Maybe painting, jewelry making, pottery and—" She tilted her head to look up at him. "Have you ever given thought to teaching photography?"

"Me?"

His expression must have looked as strained as his voice sounded, because Sunshine laughed. "Sure. Every kid in town has a camera these days, even if only the one on their cell phone."

He didn't want to lie. If he ever got his plans off the ground, she'd hear that the Hideaway had branched into wildlife photography. "Actually, that's something I've given thought to."

"Really?"

He had her full attention now. "Years ago, when I was in my late teens, I thought it would be a great idea if Hunter's Hideaway offered guided treks for aspiring wildlife photographers. You know, with workshops on the side."

"That's a wonderful idea."

He shrugged, his smile somewhat wry. "It wasn't well received by my family at the time."

"How come?"

"Well, to quote my uncle Doug… 'Look, boy, we specialize in helping hunters pack out an elk for the freezer, not take purty pictures of it.'"

He could still hear his uncle's laughter and that of Dad and Uncle Mac joining in. Even now he could clearly recall the wave of heat that had coursed up his neck and how his reddening face had egged Uncle Doug to more laughter. It had been a humiliating moment and he'd not brought up the subject of wildlife photography since then.

"That was a long time ago, Grady. Things change. I think you should do it."

"I'd like to." He let his gaze momentarily wander to where Tessa was now dragging her tennis-shoe-clad feet in the dirt, slowing herself down to a gradual stop. "But Hunter Enterprises is a family-run business, so I have to get buy-in. I'll have to prove it would attract enough business to make it worthwhile. Be a moneymaker."

"Of course it would be." She focused intently on him. "It's not as though you're suggesting the entire operation switch its emphasis solely to photography. It would be another revenue path, like the trail rides, cross-country skiing and training for high-elevation endurance riders."

"That was my thinking, too, but…" It was more complicated than she made it sound. As an adult, he now understood that better than he had as a teen. Many decisions had to be made. Youth or adult sessions or both? Weeklong or select weekends? Which seasons? How best to advertise? And he'd have to work the program around the scheduling of the cabins and property use. You couldn't have preoccupied photographers wandering during the various hunting seasons.

"Do it, Grady."

Looking into her excited eyes, a spark of determination flared in him. "So you don't think it's a far-fetched idea?"

"I think it's a great idea."

But was it one that his family wouldn't reject the moment he opened his mouth? Sunshine was right, though. With the advent of digitals, it seemed everyone had a camera and wanted to share photos with others, even if only on Facebook or Instagram.

"I admit this past summer I've given serious thought to developing a proposal. You know, to formally present to Hunter Enterprises. I've been researching and calculating how much we'd have to charge to make it profitable."

"I *love* it." Then the delight in her eyes dimmed. "But I'm disappointed that if you do this, you won't be available to teach youth classes at the Co-op. That is, if I could manage to sweet-talk you into that."

Sweet talk, hmm? What might that entail?

"Mommy! Grady! I'm on the slide now!"

Exchanging a guilty glance for having gotten engrossed in conversation, they turned to where Tessa had reached the top of a towering slide—the largest of the three—poised to push off. Gutsy little gal.

"Tessa! No! Your sleeve!"

At the terror in Sunshine's voice, his eyes locked on Tessa. But her mother's warning had come too late, for as Tessa pushed off, her laughing squeal turned to a horrified scream. The upper part of the loose jacket sleeve had snagged at the top of the slide and torn, jerking her roughly and pulling her over the edge.

Dangling.

He took off, thundering past the swings. Breath ragged. Heart pounding. His gaze never wavering from the child. But what appeared a short distance seemed to stretch into miles.

Please, God. Please.

"Mommy!"

The tearful whimper tore at his heart. And then he was suddenly there. Below her. His hands stretching high above his head in hopes of keeping her from falling should the sleeve tear free. The fabric of the buttoned jacket strained across Tessa's chest, but it wasn't choking her. Didn't inhibit her breathing.

Nevertheless, she was out of reach. "Hang on, Tessa. I'm here."

Lips trembling, she nodded as she looked down at him. And at that exact moment, seeing the unwavering trust in her eyes, something deep inside him split apart. Shaken, he looked to Sunshine, who was now at his side, offering soothing words to her daughter suspended above their heads.

"Can you climb up there, Sunshine? See if you can get the sleeve loose? Then I can catch her." He glanced down at his windbreaker. "There's a knife in that pocket. Take it in case you can't get her sleeve free."

He didn't have to tell her twice. She dipped her hand into the pocket and grasped the pocketknife. Then before he'd barely taken another breath, she was climbing the steep slide steps to the ringing sound of metal underfoot.

"Mommy?"

"Your mommy's going to get you loose, Tessa." He smiled encouragingly up at her. "Then I'm going to catch you, okay?"

"'Kay." She nodded, her eyes still filled with faith in him.

Please, Lord, let me catch her.

"I can't get it out." Sunshine's strained voice came from above him. "It's caught tight."

"Then, cut it."

But before she could get the knife pulled from its sheath, the sound of ripping fabric rent the air.

The sleeve tore loose—Tessa screaming as she dropped.

Please, God.

And then…the little girl was safe in his arms.

Heart pounding, barely able to breathe, Sunshine descended the slide steps and ran to where Grady had her daughter clasped tightly to his chest. A crying Tessa had a death grip around his neck.

Sunshine stretched out her arms and, with only a slight hesitation, Tessa loosened her hold on Grady. He lowered her to the ground where Sunshine pulled the trembling body close.

Thank God, thank God.

Whatever would she have done had Tessa been seriously hurt? Or even— No, she wouldn't go there. Not while she had the most precious possession of her heart wrapped in her arms. She tightened the embrace. *Thank You, Lord.*

A sniffling Tessa wiggled loose, pulling back to cup her mother's face in her small hands. "Don't cry, Mommy. Grady saved me."

"Yes, sweetheart, he did." Wiping away her own tears with her hand, she looked up to where he was watching them silently, his eyes filled with unmistakable relief. And something more…

"Thank you, Grady." Tears again pricked her eyes as she ran her hand along the gaping hole where the sleeve had torn away. "Tessa, you know you aren't supposed to go on the big one yet. You promised, remember?"

"I forgot, Mommy. I wanted Grady to see me go down it."

Sunshine exchanged a glance with him, catching the flinch in his expression. Her daughter's desperate hope of being noticed by a father figure had spurred her to a dangerous decision. But there would be plenty of time for chastisement later.

Grady held out a handkerchief and, with a wobbly smile, she took it from him and dabbed at her own eyes and Tessa's. Then let the little girl blow her nose.

"Looks as though you're our hero twice in one week, Grady." But the word *hero* didn't express half of what she was feeling toward him. The rush of emotion that only with willpower did she keep in check, stopping herself from leaping to her feet and throwing her arms around him, seeking solace in the strong arms that had saved her daughter.

How would she ever repay him for what he'd done for her today?

Pull out of the campaign against his mother, her conscience pricked. *Drop pursuit of compensation on your great-great-grandfather's behalf.*

Pushing aside the nagging accusations, she managed a smile. "I'll wash your handkerchief when I do laundry this week."

"No rush." He glanced behind her, his eyes narrowing. "I'll let Parks and Rec know they need to cordon off that slide until they can get it fixed. We don't want some other little kid getting clothing caught on it."

"No, the outcome might not be so fortunate." She gave Tessa another hug.

There was nothing she could do that would ever repay Grady, but surely there was a way she could demonstrate appreciation for rescuing her daughter from harm and herself from heartache. To somehow release her from the heavy weight of indebtedness to a Hunter.

Her mind raced, searching. And then, a possibility dawned.

But would he allow her to do it?

Chapter Seven

By Saturday Grady was still dealing with the impact of the rescue that left him more shaken than he cared to admit.

Too many times he'd relived—in excruciatingly detailed slow motion—that heartrending moment when he'd seen Tessa go over the edge of the slide. Again felt the fear that he wouldn't cover the distance in time to break her fall to the hard ground below.

But by God's grace, all was well.

So he should be happy, shouldn't he, that he'd see Tessa today? Her mother had called last night to ask if he could show them the historic cabins on the Hunter's Hideaway property and he'd agreed. But for a number of reasons, he was far from happy about it.

"Earth to Grady." Seated next to him, Rio bumped his shoulder with hers.

"What?" His attention jerked to the breakfast meeting underway in a conference room at the Hideaway. A roomful of curious eyes focused on him. Warmth crept into his face.

From the head of the table, his father repeated, "I asked how the game supply store is coming along."

"Extremely well." Grady met Dad's steady gaze with a reassuring nod.

At age sixty, Dave Hunter was a man who in both manner and appearance had long reminded Grady of the steady, hardworking father seen on reruns of *The Waltons* TV show. But for many years—since Luke had headed off to the army when Grady was fifteen—his father had expected more and more of his youngest son. Without fail—except for once—he'd always stepped up to deliver on those expectations.

"Even with stopping the weekend work," Grady added, "Ted and his crew are making solid headway."

"Good to hear." Dad rewarded him with a smile.

"I anticipate we'll be right on target for a mid-October opening. The security systems are being set up at both the store and the off-site storage facility. Worker bees are lined up to process online sales, including Trevor and one of his high school buddies, and a few to man the shop and demonstrate equipment. Stock is set for delivery and the website's being finalized."

Trevor, Luke's eldest child of three from his first marriage, was over-the-top excited about being a part of this new venture.

"You've done an excellent job overseeing this, Grady." Grandma Jo's eyes warmed. "We can always count on you."

"Hear, hear!" Luke, now back from his honeymoon, raised his glass of orange juice in tribute. Grady knew what effort that took. Although Luke and Dad were mending fences, it had to hurt at times that his younger brother had been running the show, heading up the enterprise alongside their father during the years he'd been gone.

"I appreciate you being my backup right now, son." His father paused, ducking his head slightly and Grady knew he was having difficulty expressing himself. "You know, freeing me up to be with your mother."

An uncomfortable silence drifted over the table.

"I'm there for you and Mom. Always." He glanced around at his extended family—grandmother, siblings, uncles, aunts and cousins. Only Mom wasn't in attendance. "We all are."

Everyone nodded. A united Hunter front.

Dad looked up again, his lips tightening as he rose from the table. "Let's get on with our day."

Once outside in the fresh mountain air, Grady climbed into his SUV and headed to his cabin. Although it was out of the way, he'd given Sunshine directions, thinking that her arrival would create less speculation if she didn't march in the front door of the Hideaway's main buildings.

As he parked outside his cabin, he paused to look at the rustic dwelling he called home. It was a relatively new cabin. Built in the late 1950s, a porch stretching across its width lent a homey look, as did half barrels of red geraniums squatting on either side of the steps. Grandma Jo's touch. What would Sunshine and Tessa think of it?

And why should he care?

Once inside, he gave his surroundings a final inspection. He'd been up late last night after Sunshine's call—vacuuming, straightening up in the living room, cleaning the kitchen and bathrooms. Making sure his clothes were gathered up from the floor and stowed neatly in closets and drawers. Opening windows to freshen things up.

He didn't often have company these days. Certainly not feminine company. He didn't want Sunshine to think he was a total slob.

He'd just hung his jacket on a peg near the front door when he heard the slamming of car doors. Female voices. Without thinking, he hastily checked his hair in an antique wall mirror in the entryway. Then, realizing what he was doing, he grimaced at himself and opened the door to welcome his guests.

"Grady!" Tessa raced up the steps to give him a hug. Which was exactly the reason why this morning's outing made him less than happy. He couldn't get attached to Sunshine's kid, nor her to him. It was one thing to pour his heart into his nieces and nephews, but past experience proved it was better to keep other people's kids at a distance.

Sunshine had told him last night that Tessa's shoulder was sore, but she seemed to be doing okay today. No worse for the wear. When she released him, she peered around him into the cabin.

"This is where you live? Can I see inside?"

"Now, Tessa—" Sunshine cast him an apologetic look.

"No problem. Come on in." At least the house was relatively clean now. Smelled good. He stepped back and, wide-eyed, Tessa joined him to take in her surroundings.

"Oh, look, Mommy!" In a flash, she covered the ground between the entry and the far side of the living room, coming to stand beside an oversize wooden rocking horse. "Can I ride it?"

"Sure." It was sturdy enough. He'd made it for Jasmine's then-four-year-old daughter, Allyson, so she'd have something to play with when they visited. There was a swing out back, too, secured to a big oak branch.

Why hadn't he gotten rid of that stuff?

"Sorry to invade your space, Grady." Sunshine stepped inside as well, looking around with as much interest as her daughter had. "This is nice. I love the open floor plan—how the staircase in the middle divides the front living area from the kitchen and dining room. It looks comfortable."

It did look nice, if he said so himself. The warmth of the wood. Sun streaming in the windows. "Well, any of the decorative stuff you can credit my sisters for. You've met Rio, who isn't much into that, but the twins between Rio and me made sure I'm not living life with lawn chairs and a card table or a wall calendar as my only artwork."

"I noticed several of your photos here." She inspected an enlargement of a doe and fawn, then looked back at him. "I've been giving some thought to your idea to incorporate a photography element at Hunter's Hideaway. How you said you're not sure where to start with a proposal. But I know exactly where you should start."

"You do?" Not surprising. She had a reputation for always having an answer and insisting others go along with it.

"It starts by addressing the main issue your family will be thinking when you approach them about it. The same thing almost every person on the planet wonders when presented with a new proposition. What's in it for me?"

"I guess I need to figure that out, don't I? I haven't been free to invest as much time on it as I'd like."

"What if I helped? For years my mother has worked at artists' cooperatives in the towns we've lived in. Jerome. Sedona. Triumph. In fact, Triumph is where Mom helped establish and still manages the local co-op. As a result, I had extensive experience working with her—which is how I landed this job."

"And that relates to my photography idea how?"

"Mom and I've helped dozens of artists prepare proposals to get their work into exclusive galleries and shops. With tons of talent out there, the competition is huge. But the artists who can present well, who can convince people that featuring their work will be worth their while…

well, they have an edge over equally talented artists who don't know how to sell themselves."

"Makes sense." The web designer for their new online store had talked about things like that. But he hadn't thought about how it might apply to his photography proposition.

"I'd be happy to help you drill down to the essence of what your family needs to know and solidify that in a proposal that will knock their socks off. So what do you say?"

From the resistance in his eyes, she'd thought Grady would flatly turn her down. But he'd said thank you and that he'd think about it.

Now, slowly bumping along a rutted dirt track that wound its way through the forest, he appeared to be giving it more thought. Asked a few questions. Grew silent. Asked a few more. So there was still hope that she could somehow balance out the debt she owed for the two rescues that week.

"Well, there it is."

Grady motioned to the left and she glimpsed an old gray cabin through a stand of ponderosas. A tingle of excitement sped through her as he pulled his SUV off the dirt road and onto an overgrown track through the trees. This was possibly the home of her great-great-grandparents. Where they'd lived. Loved. Had they started a family here? How long had they been settled before they'd lost everything to the Hunters?

When they'd climbed from the vehicle and Grady had helped Tessa out of the back, she was immediately struck by how quiet it was. An unearthly quiet, not even the sound of the wind in the trees, the bark of a squirrel or the chirp of a bird. Not so much as the distant drone of an airplane overhead. What must it have been like to have lived here over a hundred years ago, far from civilization?

An involuntary shiver curled up her spine.

As if absorbing the atmosphere of the property as well, Grady let Tessa take his hand and together they approached the weathered cabin silently.

"It's not very big, is it?" Sunshine said softly.

Likewise, Grady's voice lowered. "Not big at all."

He paused to study the cabin, then released Tessa's hand and pulled out a set of keys. Inserted them in a padlock. "We keep it locked up now. Transients found their way back here a few years ago and took up residence. They made a real mess of the place."

She didn't like the thought of someone desecrating this historic home. "That's a shame."

Tessa drew close. "Why are we whispering, Mommy?"

Sunshine smiled as Grady pushed open the door to the darkened interior. "I guess because it's so quiet here that I feel as if I need to be quiet, too."

Tessa's nose wrinkled as she eyed the open doorway with suspicion. "I don't like this place. It's creepy."

"You don't have to go inside, but stay close by, okay? Don't wander off."

Grady motioned for Sunshine to precede him into the cabin.

"Oh, wow. Dirt floors." But at least natural light came in from the small paned windows on two sides of the room, and open rafters overhead reduced the claustrophobic feeling that might otherwise have dominated. She stepped farther into the room, inspecting the chinked log walls. It was cool inside, an earthy smell mingling with the faint scent of wood smoke from past fires. She moved to the soot-stained stone fireplace, noticing the charred remains in the iron grate. "Someone's been here recently."

"Me."

She glanced at him curiously.

"I occasionally spend the night out here so I can be up early to take photos." He moved to one of the smudged windows, then looked at her again. "A twenty- or thirty-minute drive through the forest in this direction is far enough from the heart of Hideaway activity to put wild-life more at ease."

"And you said the other couple in that photo—Walter and Flora Royce—lived here? Why so far away from the current site of Hunter's Hideaway where your ancestors settled?"

He shrugged, his expression unexpectedly grim. "People needed elbow room, I guess."

She continued to survey the sparsely furnished room. A small table and chairs. Bench. Shelves. A lantern on a side table. "I don't suppose any of this is original furniture?"

"No, that's long gone."

"So where do you sleep when you come here?" A bed frame or hammock was conspicuously absent.

"Sleeping bag on the floor." He grinned at her look of dismay. "No different than camping except you have more protection from the elements and critters in here."

"True." She moved again to the fireplace, resting her hand on its cool, natural-stone surface. Had her ancestors roasted venison here? Stirred iron cooking pots of stew? Shared intimate hours in front of a crackling fire? "If only these walls could talk."

"Mommy!"

Startled at Tessa's cry of alarm, Sunshine spun toward the door. "Oh!"

Not knowing he'd come in close behind her, she'd run smack into solid-as-a-rock Grady. Startled, he gently grasped her upper arms to steady her. Heart thudding, her breath shallow, time seemed to stand still as she stared into his eyes. At the strong jaw and slightly crooked nose. He seemed to be studying her features with equal interest. And then, as if remembering what had sent her careening into him, he released her and stepped back. After only a moment's hesitation, she rushed through the open cabin door and into the bright sunlight.

Almost frantic, she searched for Tessa. "Where—?"

"Over here, Mommy!"

Aware that Grady was behind her, Sunshine hurried to where her daughter stood partially hidden, her chest pressed against a towering ponderosa, eyes wide and pointing to something on the far edge of the clearing. "What are they? Little hairy pigs?"

Some distance away, Sunshine noticed motion down low, among the shaded clumps of tall grasses and boulders. Then, warily, two small creatures emerged and she recognized them at once.

"Javelina." Grady's low voice echoed her thoughts.

Tessa stared up at him. "Have-a-what?"

"Javelina," he repeated, amusement lighting his eyes. "And yes, they do look like hairy pigs, but they're not pigs."

Sunshine eyed them warily. "They don't usually come out during the daytime, do they?"

"Actually, they can be quite active in the mornings and enjoy sunshine. They don't usually venture into elevations a whole lot higher than the Mogollon Rim, though, so these may have gotten separated from their herd."

"Let's leave them in peace, then, shall we? We need to let you get back to work, so the other cabin can wait for another time."

"Work will be there waiting whenever I return."

"What is it, exactly, that you do at Hunter's Hideaway?" She'd been wanting to ask for some time.

"Your question would probably be better stated as what *don't* I do at the Hideaway." He reached for Tessa's hand and the threesome moved back toward the cabin and his vehicle. "You name it and at some time or another I've probably done it."

"But what do you do now?"

"I don't exactly have a title." His forehead creased as he helped Tessa into the backseat and secured her in. "I was about fifteen when Luke took off for the army, and ever since then I've been Dad's right-hand man. Dad's the eldest of his siblings, so after the death of his father, by default he became the primary overseer of the Hideaway. And by default, too, I guess, I'm following in his footsteps."

He chucked a giggling Tessa under the chin, then shut the back door and leaned against it, arms folded.

"My days vary. Overseeing property maintenance and supervising—along with Rio and our cousin J.C.—horse care, trail rides and horse and rider training programs. Helping hunters pack in their trophies. Providing support and guidance on inn and general store operation." With a laugh, he took an exaggerated breath and continued, "I order supplies. Manage employees. Keep on top of the events master calendar, provide preseason scouting tips for hunters and mingle with our varied guests. I guess you'd say I'm a troubleshooter, involved in every aspect of the business."

"I'm impressed."

"And in the midst of all that, I managed to pick up an associate's degree in business at Northland Pioneer College and rounded that out with additional online classes for a bachelor's." With a proud grin, he pushed away from the truck to pull keys from his pocket. "Give me a minute to lock up, okay? Then I'd be happy to come back to do some more bragging. It's always sweet to impress a pretty girl."

Laughing, she took a playful swat at him, but missed him by a mile.

When he returned, he climbed into the driver's seat next to her, slammed the door and started up the SUV.

"Fortunately, Luke's now taking on additional responsibilities for the Hideaway. Correspondence and paperwork to keep us legal with federal, state and county agencies. Overseeing financial investments. Can't say I'll miss doing that."

He gave her a lopsided grin and for some silly reason, her cheeks warmed.

"He'll also make sure," Grady added, "that we have facts and figures for making critical decisions."

She studied him thoughtfully, trying not to notice his still twinkling eyes. "So that means he'll be a primary person you'll need to convince that your photography idea is feasible?"

"I guess so." He frowned as he turned the vehicle in the direction from which they'd come. "Our relationship was strained when he first got out of the army six years ago. He and Dad had a falling-out back in the day. Then when he returned, here I am filling the shoes our father always intended for him to fill. We've pretty much worked through it, but sometimes it still gets thorny."

"Do you think he'll push back because he's now in a position to?"

"I don't think so." He thought a moment longer, eyes narrowing as they bumped down the rub-board road. "But it might not be a half-bad idea to bring someone on board who knows how to deal with that possibility."

He slanted a look at her. Then winked.

"Know anyone who might have that type of experience?"

Chapter Eight

It turned out, however, to be far easier to convince Grady to take her up on her offer of assistance than it was to find a time and place suitable for them to work on the project together.

Thankfully, Tori was available to babysit, or they probably never would have worked things out with their busy schedules. Which might have meant they'd have had to work via phone and email.

Considering how nervous she was after dinner Tuesday evening as she readied for the drive to Grady's place, working by phone might have been the better option.

Tori stepped back to look at her approvingly. "Pretty skirt, Sunshine."

"Do you think it's too much?" She hadn't worn the striking Native American patterned wool skirt topped by a burgundy suede fringed jacket since last winter. But mid-September evenings were cooling down. "I want to look—"

"Beautiful?" Tori's eyes glowed with approval. "You nailed it."

Sunshine made a face. "No, I meant professional."

"Well, you look that, too."

"I'm thinking of wearing this a week from Friday to that parent-teacher meeting, so I want to see if I still feel comfortable in it. It'll be the first kickoff event for the town council elections, with each candidate given an opportunity to briefly state our platform and answer questions."

"Three of you, right?"

"Right. Irv Baydlin. Elaine Hunter. Me."

"Does Grady ever mention that when you're with him? I mean, does he say anything about you running against his mother?"

"Not so far."

"Seems like an elephant in the room to me. And now with what I found online this morning, *two* elephants."

After days of diligently searching, Tori had unearthed documentation that Sunshine's great-grandmother's maiden name had been Royce. Which meant that she'd most likely confirm her parents were Walter and Flora.

"I have to admit, it's hard not to tell him that I'm almost ninety-nine percent certain the owners of the cabin he showed me on Saturday are my ancestors."

Tori folded her arms, her expression doubtful. "Do you think it's wise to withhold that? I mean, the guy saved you and your daughter twice. Now you're trying to repay that debt by spending more time with him on this business-proposal thing. Don't you think he might resent it when you pop up with a big 'reveal'? Why not tell him now? Why keep it a secret?"

Sunshine slipped her feet into a pair of black pumps. "Because until we can find unquestionable evidence that the Hunters somehow managed to cheat my great-greats out of their land, there's no point in bringing it up."

"So the elephant in the room grows ever larger."

"You're as bad as Tessa, Tori. You worry too much. See imaginary things in the closet."

"Someone needs to. And I do it because I care."

Sunshine gave her friend a grateful look. "I care about you, too. But everything is going to be fine. One more step back and you'll confirm the names of my great-great-grandparents. Then we can decide where to go from there on proving the rest of it. Are you on board?"

"I guess so. But I don't want to see you—or this Grady guy—get hurt."

"Nobody's going to get hurt." How could they? They hardly knew each other. Staring into each other's eyes when she'd bumped into him at the cabin had been nothing but awkward. Besides, it wasn't as if she intended to sue his family for what they'd done to her predecessors. She'd present the evidence and leave it in the hands of God—and the consciences of the Hunters.

But tonight she had to keep her focus on the business at hand—lifting some of the weight of indebtedness off her shoulders by doing a good turn for Grady.

The two hours flew by faster than he could ever have imagined, with Sunshine seated on one side of a corner of the dining table, him the other, so they could share a view of his laptop screen. But in presenting to her the research he'd gathered over the past few months, it didn't appear to be as compelling as he'd built it up in his mind to be. She asked good questions, though, that provoked him to think more deeply, to look at the issues from a different angle.

He glanced at the attractive woman, sweet smelling and feminine in that soft jacket, the fringe of which—like the sway of her hair—caught his attention every time she moved. "What do you think, Sunshine? Can I build a winning case?"

If she said no, what was the point in trying? Luke, with his financial savvy, would eat him up and spit him out.

She leaned back in her chair. "If you can fill in those gaps, I think the bones of it are here."

"I can squeeze in a few hours for gap filling this week."

"When that's done, we'll group your data into logical segments, sort of how I've illustrated on the newsprint pad here. Then we'll give thought to the sequencing and break each down into bite-size, presentable pieces. You have to hit them out of the gate with a 'big promise' punch, then the remainder of the presentation will back up your promises."

"You make this sound simple."

"Simple doesn't mean without considerable thought or planning, though. I think you've done a lot of that. We need to tweak what you have."

She was probably just being nice, careful not to be overly critical of his hodgepodge of notes. But it was far better to have her punch holes in what he'd been thinking now than to have Luke go after him on those same points in front of the whole family.

"So how are you feeling about this, Grady? Have I hijacked your plans? Veered off from the direction you intended to go?"

"No, not at all." He rose from his chair and stretched. "It's as if you've taken my vague, cloudy dreams and solidified them in my own mind and, hopefully, in the minds of my family members in the future."

She looked relieved. Had she been concerned that he wouldn't care for her input? He much preferred dealing with a straight shooter than someone who only said what they thought he wanted to hear. Which might actually make her a solid candidate for the town council if she could somehow clearly reveal that side of herself to voters.

She wouldn't win, of course. Not with Mom in the race, but still...

He moved into the kitchen to look inside the refrigerator. "Would you like something to drink? A snack, maybe?"

"Thanks, but I need to be going." Sunshine stood and reached for the purse she'd looped over the back of her chair. "I want to make sure Tessa hasn't given Tori problems getting her settled down for the night."

"She's still thinking there are mysterious things in the closet? I can understand after the fall from a slide how that might add to her anxiety."

"Oddly, that didn't seem to compound the situation. In fact, she seems to be more focused on you as her hero than reliving those scary moments."

"That's good, I guess." But he didn't want to be any little kid's hero. What had Jasmine's daughter thought when he'd broken up with her mom? He'd been her hero, too, but what scars had been left when he'd abruptly disappeared from the child's life? That was when he'd vowed to never get involved again with a woman who had children.

Although he wasn't *involved* with Sunshine, he had come in contact with her daughter several times last week. Dangerous territory for a little kid's heart.

A man's, too.

As he walked her to the door, he couldn't help looking at Sunshine with regret. Too bad she had a kid. Too bad as well that she was running against his mother for a town council seat.

Sunshine's smile dissolved as she looked up at him.

"Why so glum? You've got a fantastic idea, Grady. You've done your homework. All we have to do is put the puzzle pieces together to make a complete picture for your family."

"I can't thank you enough for your input tonight." He mustered a smile. "I promise I'll have those gaps you talked about filled as fast as I can."

"Wonderful." Her eyes sparkled as she looked up at him, and for a long moment their gazes locked.

His mouth went dry. She was beautiful standing there in the dim light of the entryway, her silky black hair shiny and her smooth skin appearing soft, touchable. Heart drumming against the walls of his chest, he swallowed. Then, pulling himself together, he abruptly jerked open the front door—only to find his cousin, Pastor Garrett McCrae, standing there under the porch light, hand raised to knock.

"Good evening, Sunshine. Grady." Garrett's smile was way too wide as he took in the pair standing inside the entry. "Hope I'm not interrupting anything."

"I'm on my way out." Sunshine glanced uncertainly at Grady. "I'll see you later?"

"Call me when you get home so I know you're there safely."

Her brows rose, but she nodded. Then with a smile directed at Garrett, she slipped past him and into the shadows to her car. Grady waited in the doorway until she drove off, then motioned his cousin inside.

"To what honor do I owe this house call, Garrett?"

"I haven't seen you for a while except in church, so thought I'd stop by and keep a fellow lonely old bachelor company." He plopped himself on the sofa and stretched out as Grady eased himself into a nearby recliner. "But it looks as though things may have taken an interesting turn since we last talked."

Grady grunted. "Don't go getting any wild ideas. Ms. Carston was here on business. Nothing more. You can wipe that silly grin off your face."

Garrett's gray eyes questioned, but Grady didn't feel like enlightening him any further. Although there was a four-year age gap between them, they'd long been buds, but he didn't intend to share his hopes for the photography addition to the Hunter's Hideaway lineup with him. Not yet anyway. Maybe closer to the presentation he'd call on the good pastor to offer up prayers on his behalf.

Straightening up, Garrett glanced around him, a puzzled expression on his face. Then he looked past Grady and into the dining room. "Something's different."

"Nothing's different."

"Wait a minute!" Laughter lit Garrett's features. "You cleaned, didn't you? Not just ran a vacuum and sprayed air freshener, but you picked things up, stashed the junk someplace and actually *cleaned.*"

Garrett leaped to his feet and started across the room.

"Hey! Where do you think you're going?"

"To inspect the bathroom."

In spite of himself, Grady couldn't help cracking a smile. "Get back here."

Still laughing, Garrett resettled himself on the sofa. "I can't believe this. I imagine you haven't cleaned this place much since you booted Jas—"

Grady's warning look cut him off. "Don't go there."

"Well, it's the truth, isn't it?"

Grady didn't want to talk about truth. Or have his housecleaning efforts speculated upon. "So what are you really doing here tonight, Garrett?"

The laughter dimmed in his cousin's eyes as he leaned

forward to rest his forearms on his knees. "I wanted to talk to you about your mother."

Grady flipped the recliner lever and brought himself upright. "What about Mom?"

Garret looked him steadily in the eye.

"My mom—" Meaning Grady's dad's sister, his aunt Suzy. "My mom told me your dad wants Aunt Elaine to drop out of the election."

Grady's throat tightened. "Why?"

Was there something about her condition his parents weren't sharing with their kids? Last he'd talked to his mother, not even twenty-four hours ago, she was gung ho for the campaign trail. She viewed this time-out as temporary.

"He thinks it's going to be too much for her. Too much stress right when she needs to be resting and focusing on fighting the cancer."

"You should know my mother well enough to recognize that Dad spouting off his opinion isn't going to sway her. Once she sets her mind to something, just try to bar the door."

"Despite good intentions, chemo treatments can take a toll, Grady. She's barely getting underway with it. Even in a small town like this, elections are demanding. They take time and effort, putting yourself out there nonstop in the public eye. Which is another thing—her immune system will be compromised, so she'll have to be extra careful with cold and flu season getting underway."

"This is a reelection, though." Grady relaxed somewhat. "Everybody knows her. Knows what she stands for. She could spend the next seven weeks in utter seclusion and still win."

"Maybe."

"What exactly are you hinting at, Garrett?" He didn't like this beating-around-the-bush stuff.

"This election is a little different."

"How so?"

"Irvin's doing his best to mount up a strong opposition, promising this and that to folks who pretty much are looking for a handout wherever they turn. People who'd like to see the high-and-mighty Hunters toppled. You do realize, don't you, that we've had a family member on the town council since the town's founding in the 1920s?"

"And Sunshine?" Garrett continued. "Like I told you earlier, she's been all over the place in the past few weeks since that friend of hers came to town. She's not sitting around naively assuming the artists in the community can get her elected. She knows there aren't enough of them to do that."

"I don't see how any of this will make a difference."

"Live in your rose-colored-glasses world, Grady, but my mom is concerned. Dad, too. Especially if your dad persuades your mother to give it up."

"He won't."

Garrett fell silent for a moment, and then he cocked his head, his gaze boring into Grady's. "There *is* such a thing as a write-in vote."

"Meaning?"

"If your mother pulls out, we could mount a campaign to get *you* elected in Aunt Elaine's stead. You won't be on the ballot, but you could still pull it off."

Think again, cuz. Grady resolutely pushed himself out of the recliner and pointed a warning finger at his cousin. "No."

"Why not? You don't think your lady friend can beat you, do you?"

"Sunshine is not my 'lady friend.' And I'm not much

concerned about whether or not she could beat me because I'm not running for an elected office." His eyes narrowed. "Why don't *you* do it if you're worried about Hunters losing?"

"Because you have to be a resident for at least one year prior to the election. I moved back here last December and I have no idea how much longer I'll hold this interim pastor position. Besides, I have my hands full at Christ's Church."

"And my hands aren't full, too? I can't take on a four-year commitment." Grady spread his arms wide. "What do you think I've been doing around the Hideaway since I was a teenager anyway?"

"You mean besides sneaking off for a kissing fest with some cute little gal?" Garrett teased, an attempt to ease a heated moment.

Grady couldn't help but laugh. His cousin hadn't exactly been a choir boy in his younger days, either. "You should talk, preacher."

Garrett suppressed a smile. "Honestly, Grady, if you'd be willing to give this serious thought, I think it would ease my folks' minds. Uncle Doug's, too. Probably the whole family's."

"I'm not running for office." And he wasn't praying about it, either, so Garrett better not ask him to.

With a sound of frustration, Garrett stood at the same moment the phone rang. "Better get that. Your lady friend's checking in."

"I told you—"

"I know. She's not your lady friend." Garrett headed to the front door, then paused to look back. "But you'll be careful, won't you? I don't want to be the last bachelor left standing in the Hunter clan."

Chapter Nine

"This is looking good, Grady."

Sunshine motioned to the laptop screen as she pushed her chair back from Grady's dining table. This was their fourth work session over the past two weeks, and progress had been steady.

"You think we're getting there?"

"Definitely."

After what had felt like a too-close encounter right before Garrett had shown up at the conclusion of their first meeting, she'd been hesitant to meet with Grady again. But she hadn't felt ill at ease during the follow-up sessions at all. Not to say that Grady wasn't Grady. He'd probably flirted in the hospital nursery on the very day of his arrival into the world. He couldn't help himself now any more than he could back then. Which actually made for a fun and nonthreatening time together.

Tonight, though, while not awkward in that respect, Grady seemed preoccupied.

As had become their custom when they'd wrapped things up for the night, he rose to pour himself a mug of coffee and her a cup of tea, then led the way to the living room. She followed, pulling a crocheted afghan across her lap as she made herself comfortable on the sofa. He settled into the recliner and she clasped her hands around the warm teacup.

She'd come to look forward to this time to talk about various topics, to get to know each other better. Grady was an intriguing man despite being a Hunter.

"I could put a fire in the fireplace if you're chilly." He started to rise, but she shook her head.

"No, I'm fine. But thanks. The afghan's all I need."

"You're sure?"

"Positive."

He eased back down and took a sip of coffee. "I'm pleased with the way the proposal is coming together. Thanks to you. What do you think? Can we finalize it at our next meeting?"

Only one more? An unexpected wave of disappointment washed through her. "I think so. I'll polish up the slide presentation I've been working on and we can put the final touches on it."

"If my family doesn't go for this after all the work we've put into it, I should probably saddle up and ride off into the sunset."

She leaned forward. "They'll go for it, Grady."

"I hope so."

"This means a lot to you, doesn't it?"

He set his mug on the end table next to him. "It's something I've wanted to pursue ever since I got into photography as a teenager. A dream that never died."

She couldn't help but smile as he glanced away, almost as if he'd revealed too much of himself in that simple statement.

"I can't see why they would turn this down now." She took another sip of the fragrant tea. "There's minimal financial investment. Negligible advertising expense, too, because it will be incorporated into the Hideaway's other promotional efforts—brochures and the website. It's mostly juggling around cabin availability and hunting seasons. I think your documentation proves it will be profitable."

He gave her a regretful smile. "With my family, I learned long ago not to get too excited about something until it's a done deal."

"Getting excited is half the fun. But if for some totally irrational reason they reject your proposal, that doesn't have to be the end of it."

"What do you mean?"

"Hunter's Hideaway isn't the only game in town. Or at least not the only game in Arizona mountain country. Or anywhere for that matter. There are plenty of other outdoor-related businesses that might welcome a potential moneymaker like this, one that has a business plan mapped out and ready to go."

He looked at her as if she'd lost her mind.

"Your family doesn't hold the key to your dream, Grady. God does. And if He leads you elsewhere…"

His brows lowered. "I can't imagine taking this elsewhere."

"I'm not saying you should. I'm pointing out that you have options. Don't close doors. That's God's job."

He rose from the recliner, then moved to place a hand on the polished oak mantel of the stone fireplace, where he stared into the cold grate, deep in thought. Under the surface all evening, he'd been restless. Agitated. It wasn't her imagination.

"There's something bothering you, isn't there?" she said softly. "Something that doesn't have anything to do with your business proposal."

His head jerked up in surprise, and then he nodded almost imperceptibly.

"Yeah. Something that makes this proposal seem inconsequential."

"I'm a good listener."

"I know. And it's something you'll find out tomorrow anyway. I just didn't know how to tell you." He fisted the hand he'd placed on the fireplace mantel. "It's not easy for me to talk about."

Curious—and somewhat alarmed—she set her cup aside, then pulled the afghan more closely around herself to wait. To give him time to work through whatever was troubling him.

The antique clock on the mantel ticked loudly, measuring the seconds. Overhead a wind-loosened pinecone hit the rooftop. The refrigerator's steady hum silenced.

Then with a heavy sigh, Grady looked to her again, his eyes bleak. "My mother has breast cancer."

With a gasp, she momentarily pressed her hand to her mouth. "Oh, Grady. I'm sorry."

With a guilty sense of self-incrimination, she chastised herself for the appalling first thoughts that had flashed uninvited into her mind. Would Elaine pull out of the election? Would her opponents now have a chance to win?

Forgive me, Lord.

A sad smile touched his lips, tugging at her heart. "We found out a day or two before Luke and Delaney's wedding. We didn't know the extent of it then, of course. But she wouldn't let them postpone the wedding or call off the honeymoon."

She waited in silence, praying for Grady. His mother. His family.

"Anyway, it was a family decision not to say anything to anyone until we knew more. She had surgery. Then a reaction to meds. Council members, of course, were informed in private that she'd miss a few sessions due to a needed medical procedure. But the word *cancer* wasn't shared with anyone outside the family."

"And now?"

"She started chemo a week or so ago and it's already taking its toll much faster than she anticipated. She's really sick." He pushed away from the fireplace and slowly paced the room. "So tomorrow she'll make it public that she's battling cancer. She feels because she holds a public office that the community is entitled to know."

"What a blow to your mother and your family."

He nodded. "But that's not all I need to tell you."

What more could there be?

"Mom wants to remain on the ballot." He forced a smile. "That's so typical of her. She doesn't want to let down those who voted her into office and want to see her remain there."

Sunshine winced. And *she* was doing her best to unseat his mother from a second term.

"Which leads me to inform you—" Grady halted his pacing and rammed his hands into his jeans' back pockets, his blue eyes piercing into hers. "Mom's asked me to stand in for her tomorrow night at the parent-teacher meeting. In her absence I'll present her platform, her point of view, her hopes for Hunter Ridge."

Sunshine sucked in a startled breath.

She'd be behind the podium with Grady Hunter?

"Well, don't you look dolled up and ready to dance." Luke leaned against the door frame of Grady's office Friday evening, a smirk on his face.

Grady's lip curled as Grandma Jo adjusted his tie.

"Don't you have someplace you need to be, Luke? Like giving your new bride a little attention?"

"Now, boys." Enveloped in her fuzzy blue bathrobe, Mom looked up from where she sat at his desk, going through her notes and drilling him on her election platform. Dark shadows emphasized the weariness in her eyes, belying the amused smile. He still couldn't get used to her in that colorful turban she'd donned, having had her head shaved in anticipation of losing her hair to the chemo. It was all Mom could do to keep Rio from shaving her own head as a solidarity move. "I think Grady looks quite handsome."

At least he'd talked her out of a suit. Who wore suits in Hunter Ridge except when getting married or buried? But she'd insisted he pair up a tie with a tan, corduroy sports jacket and a new pair of jeans.

As he'd reminded her earlier, though, he wasn't the one running for office. It was important he make that clear after what Garrett had shared with him about Aunt Suzy and Uncle Mac wanting him to be a write-in candidate. No way.

"Yep, Mom," Luke agreed. "My baby brother looks mighty fine tonight. Even shaved. Combed his hair, too."

"Enough." Grandma Jo pointed at the door. "We have more we need to pour into Grady's head before he leaves for the parent-teacher meeting."

"Shouldn't be a problem." Luke's eyes twinkled. "There's plenty of empty space in there."

"Out." Grandma laughingly marched up to Luke, turned him toward the hallway and gave him a gentle push. Shut the door behind him. Still smiling, she shook her head at her daughter-in-law. "I don't think your boys will ever grow up."

"So how are you feeling about this now, Grady?" His mother set aside her notes to study him.

He adjusted his tie. "I don't understand why this falls to me. It's not as though this family has a shortage of members to choose from."

"You know we've always counted on you," Grandma Jo reminded, a proud look in her eyes.

Wasn't that the truth? *Luke has a tiff with Dad and bails on Hunter's Hideaway, so guess who's enlisted to take his place? Dad prefers the manual labor and, consequently, who gets stuck with the endless paperwork? Uncle Doug hates contract negotiations, so their go-to guy takes that on, as well.*

Given a minute or two, he could tick off dozens more let-Grady-do-it scenarios that had landed on his plate over the years. Stuff that he'd never, at the time, given a thought to as he'd taken them on. But it had begun to dawn on him, when he'd found it hard to fit in a few measly hours with Sunshine each week, that his life revolved exclusively around Hunter's Hideaway.

"You've told the whole family no one related to the Hunters is to show up there, right? It's just me—solo." He didn't want family members watching from the sidelines. He'd be uncomfortable enough playing politician in front of strangers—even as a stand-in.

"Yes, we got the word out."

While that was a relief, he still didn't look forward to fulfilling his familial duties. Forty minutes later, his brain stuffed to the max with information from his mom, he headed to town. When he stepped through the door of the high school cafeteria, he couldn't help but look for Sunshine.

And there she was. Across the room chatting with Mayor Vicky Silas, a hardworking, gray-haired descendant of one of the earlier families to settle Hunter Ridge. Sunshine, dressed in that eye-catching print skirt she'd worn the first night she'd come to his place, almost glowed as the high school principal stepped in to join them. The same principal who'd on occasion hauled Grady into his office for rowdy behavior.

Glancing quickly away, he spied other teachers, school board members and parents he recognized, including several members of the artisan community. It looked to be a healthy turnout.

Not far away, candidate Irvin Baydlin—who'd also known Grady as a boy—was engaged in conversation with several teachers who Grady recognized as having, at one time or another, taught his nieces and nephews. And—good grief—wasn't that Mrs. Rivers? His seventh-grade English teacher who'd constantly been on him for poor spelling and less-than-perfect grammar?

It looked as though Mom picked the wrong Hunter for tonight's assignment.

"Grady!"

He pivoted toward a gal his brother had dated in high school, relieved at seeing a familiar face that didn't remind him of his past wrongdoings. She was married and a math teacher now.

"Hey, Monica. Good to see you."

"You, too." Then the corners of her mouth dipped downward as she gave his arm a squeeze. "I'm sorry to hear about your mother."

"Keep her in your prayers." He'd expected to hear words of concern tonight, but he hadn't adequately prepared himself to discuss Mom's illness. It was too new. Too raw. He glanced around the spacious room. "Do you know where I'm supposed to go? I'm filling in for my mother tonight."

"That's what I'd heard." She pointed to the stage, where a table, five folding chairs and podium had been set up. And in front of them, on the cafeteria floor, were several dozen chairs, as well. "The candidates—and you, too, of course—will be up there."

He willed himself not to grimace. He'd hoped for a more informal setting where he could relax into a casual conversation. This was too much like a speech.

He didn't do speeches.

"Give your mother my love." Monica patted his arm, then stepped away to greet someone entering the door behind him.

He set a course for the stage as those around him began to fill the seats on the main floor, and had just reached the steps when Sunshine appeared at his side.

"Nervous, Grady?"

"Not really." Would lightning strike him for that blatant fib? "How about you?"

"Yes!" She laughed as he motioned for her to precede him onto the stage. It was easy to see how she came by her nickname with that smile warming him from the inside out. "I've never spoken in front of a group this big."

"You'll do fine."

Her expression sobered and they moved toward the chairs arranged for them. "How is your mother?"

"It's rough. But she insists if this is what she has to go through to come out on the other side and live a long, meaningful life, she'll do it without complaint."

"She's courageous. Has a deep faith."

"She's all that." An invisible fist tightened around his heart. "But she's realistically aware that faith isn't a ticket to always getting what you want. Earthly life has an expiration date. A shorter one for some than others."

They'd barely seated themselves when Irvin, accompanied by the president of the parent-teacher organization and the head of the school board, joined them. The latter introduced them to the audience then, with an encouraging smile from Sunshine, Grady rose to make his mom's presentation.

Twenty minutes later he was done and, relieved, he settled himself back into his chair. A few people had asked general questions, which he felt confident in answering. Because Elaine Hunter was the incumbent, most knew her and her track record by reputation. He'd gotten off easy.

It was rougher for Sunshine.

She'd approached the podium with apparent confidence despite her confession of nervousness. In addition to being the prettiest one on stage, she made a good showing by focusing her ten-minute presentation on issues related to the community as a whole—education, increased employment opportunities, the environment—rather than solely on the concerns of local artists.

Please get her through the questions, Lord.

That was the hardest part, not knowing what challenges might come out of left field when someone raised a hand. Friend or foe? As he'd expected, being a resident of Hunter Ridge for a mere two years and known as outspoken on behalf of the artisan community, questions directed at her were more pointed and probing than they'd been with him. But, fortunately, none were overtly hostile. When she sat down thirty minutes later, he sensed in her a relief equal to his own and gave her a reassuring wink.

Irvin, though, seemed determined to make it clear that neither Elaine Hunter nor Sunshine Carston had a realistic grasp of the needs of Hunter Ridge.

A pompous man in a loud jacket and sporting a bow

tie, he didn't merely present an overview of the platform he had chosen to run on. Instead, he managed to take digs at his opponents, even going as far, under the guise of expressing sympathy at Grady's mother's "unfortunate health setback," to raise questions as to her fitness to continue serving in public office. Mom had warned him to expect that, to not react, so he was prepared to keep his expression deliberately neutral.

But when Irvin, in occasional humorous asides, focused his sights on Sunshine, it was all Grady could do not to toss the guy off the stage. Referring to her with a patronizing smile as "our junior candidate," he proceeded to poke holes in her presentation by twisting her words and leaving his listeners with the impression that what Irvin was saying she'd said was in reality what she'd meant.

Blood boiling, Grady kept his features schooled to bland indifference, but a covert glance in Sunshine's direction confirmed her mortification. Not so much in her expression, which remained pleasant and seemingly unaffected by Irvin's gibes, but by something Grady couldn't put his finger on. Something more subtle he was picking up on, having gotten to know her better these past few weeks.

After forty minutes Irvin finally shut his trap and sat down. Then the president of the parent-teacher organization said a few closing words and encouraged attendees to linger and meet the candidates in person.

"This has been the longest night of my life," Sunshine whispered as he escorted her from the stage.

But before he could respond with more than a shared glance of mutual sympathy, they were drawn off to separate conversations with potential voters. An hour later, he saw Sunshine slip out and started in that direction himself, hoping to have a few words with her in the parking lot.

Unfortunately, Irvin intercepted him. But before he could speak whatever was on his mind, Grady took the lead.

"You had some good points there, Mr. Baydlin, but wouldn't you agree you overstepped?"

"In what way?"

"This is Hunter Ridge. We can afford to show our opponents common courtesy."

"I believe voters have a right to know that your mother's health may affect her fulfilling her duties."

"That remains to be seen. Treatments have barely started. But that's not what I'm referring to."

"Which is?"

"The digs at Sunshine Carston were uncalled-for. This wasn't a forum intended for personal attacks."

"I hardly consider clarifying what another candidate has publically said to be a personal attack."

"What would you call deliberately twisting someone's words to suit your own agenda when there's no opportunity for rebuttal?"

Irvin chuckled. "It's obvious you're not well schooled in campaign strategies, young man. You have to seize opportunities when they arise. Obviously, you need to leave the politicking to your mother."

"My mother wouldn't have given her blessing to your treatment of Ms. Carston, and you know it."

"So tell me again—" Irvin pushed open the exit door and stepped into the night, his eyes narrowing as he looked back at Grady in open speculation. "Which candidate is it you're campaigning for?"

Chapter Ten

❧

"It's been days since that parent-teacher meeting," Sunshine told jewelry maker Benton Mason as they rearranged the Co-op gallery's display cases. "Yet I can still hear Irvin's barbed remarks. The way he twisted my words."

"You knew what you might be getting into," the heavy-set bearded man reminded, "when you were asked to represent the artisan community in the town council race."

She carefully lifted the sculpture of a—well, she wasn't exactly sure what it was. But it had an interesting texture and pleasing lines that drew the eye. "I suppose. But at the time I filed, Elaine Hunter was the lone candidate. She would never have publicly sliced and diced me like Irvin did. There wasn't an opportunity to challenge his assertions."

"You'll get that at this Friday's engagement with the veterans' group."

She did *not* look forward to that. "I won't play dirty like Irvin."

"You don't have to." Benton moved the heavy pedestal several feet away, under more direct lighting, and she placed the sculpture once again atop it. "My wife and I thought you did great last week. You presented your ideas well. Came across as reasonable and civic minded. Gave voters the opportunity to see that the artists new to this community aren't the enemy."

She grimaced. "Then Irvin twisted everything I said and left them with a totally different impression."

"You underestimate those in attendance." He nodded to an acrylic still life on a nearby easel and she lifted it down so he could move the tripod stand. "I sensed a discomfort around me when Baydlin starting taking potshots at you. Oh, sure, some will listen to what he said and form an opinion in his favor without examining the facts. But not all. Far from all."

"I hope you're right."

"You need to toughen up, Sunshine." He took the canvas from her and placed it back on the newly relocated easel. He knew all about toughening up, having served in the armed forces and now working through PTSD-related issues. "Only five weeks until voters hit the polls. It may get rough."

She wrinkled her nose. "I don't think I'm cut out for this."

"Sure you are. I have every confidence in you. You're passionate about meeting the needs of the community, not just the artists. You have a strong sense of right and wrong. A zeal for justice." Benton placed his hands on his hips. "Baydlin took potshots at Elaine Hunter, too, remember? About her health and how she won't keep her commitments if she wins the election. How she's not currently keeping her commitment to the town council."

"That was nasty."

"Do you think it was easy for Grady Hunter to sit there and listen to that?"

"I guess not." She reached for a feather duster and brushed the top of a glass counter.

"Of course not. But I did see him speaking to Irvin after you left. By the look on their faces, he may have been clearing the air in private. At some point you may need to do that with Irvin, too."

"And let him use that against me in a public forum, as well?"

"Hey." He touched her arm and she faced him. "When you were asked by the Artists' Co-op members to run for office, did you pray about it at all?"

"Of course."

"And the answer was…?"

"That getting elected to the town council was a long shot, but I might educate the community about the needs of newcomers to town who earn a living with their artwork."

"And has that calling changed?"

"I guess not."

"It's not about winning, Sunshine. But you know that."

She did. Despite Elaine's health being in question, Grady's mother was the favored candidate. Sunshine had known that from the start. Irvin filing to run and his less-than-courteous campaigning had caused her to lose focus, her sense of purpose.

"Now, didn't you have errands to run this afternoon? I have things covered here."

"Thank you. And thanks for the pep talk."

She ran upstairs to her apartment, paused to see if Tori had made headway on her family research—she'd sent off email queries to county and state offices to follow a few leads—then grabbed a jacket to ward off the chill. October already. That seemed impossible.

Once outside the gallery, she noticed Grady's SUV

parked in front of the neighboring wild game supply store, the shop's door standing open. Unlike most days, though, there was no sound of pounding and sawing, so thankfully that phase might be over. She'd see Grady tonight—for a final review of the presentation slides— but should she stop in to say hello now?

She'd taken a few steps in that direction when a gruff male voice called her name, drawing her to a halt. A glowering Gideon Edlow, bundled up against the wind, crossed the road and came to stand in front of her.

"Hello, Gideon."

Not much taller than she was, the talented potter eyed her with distaste, a wisp of a mustache and the goatee on his pointed chin almost trembling with suppressed outrage.

"For someone who's a candidate for the town council, you sure are hard to get hold of." He rammed his hands into his jacket pockets. "I've stopped by the Co-op gallery numerous times the past several days and you're either occupied with customers or gallivanting off somewhere. Like now."

She tensed. Accommodating customers and taking time to run errands or meet with community members was unacceptable? "You should have left a message. I would have returned your call."

"I'd prefer to speak with you face-to-face."

"What's on your mind, then?"

"For one thing, you've gotten awfully cozy with your town council opponents."

"Irvin Baydlin and I are real buds."

Gideon's mouth twisted. "I'm talking about Elaine Hunter's son, not that pompous slime, Baydlin. I don't consider him competition even after that speech of his at the parent-teacher meeting."

Gideon had attended? She hadn't seen him. He wasn't a parent or a teacher, so he must have been lurking in the shadows.

Suddenly conscious of the open door to the adjacent store, she lowered her voice, hoping Gideon would follow her cue. "For a few weeks Mr. Hunter will be representing his mother at gatherings hosted for the candidates. I'm sure I'll see him and Mr. Baydlin often between now and election day. I intend to keep interactions friendly. But I would hardly call that 'getting cozy.'"

Gideon *had* seen her, though, visiting with Grady at the park the day he'd rescued Tessa from the slide mishap. How long might he have lingered out of sight to watch them? They hadn't done anything inappropriate or incriminating. Surely he didn't know of their meetings at Grady's place. Did he?

"I don't think you understand what's at stake here, Sunshine." To her alarm, he didn't keep his voice down. "You've lived in Hunter Ridge two years. I've lived here five and, believe me, people in this town have kicked me around more times than I can count. Put me down because I choose to make my way in the world by adding beauty to it. Not marching around in the wilderness with a gun, bow or fishing rod."

She winced as he jerked his head in the direction of Grady's new store.

"I'm aware," she said quietly, again hoping he'd follow suit, "that the artists in this community face numerous challenges. And I think you'd have to agree that I've taken a lead in attempting to bridge that gap, to approach the town council numerous times on behalf of our segment of the population."

Not merely bellyaching like Gideon was known to do.

The man snorted. "And where's that gotten us? No-

We'd like to send you two free books from the series you are enjoying now. Your two books have a combined cover price of over $10 retail, but are yours to keep absolutely FREE! We'll even send you two wonderful surprise gifts. You can't lose!

Each of your FREE books is filled with joy, faith and traditional values as and women open their hearts to each other and join together on a spiritu journey.

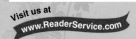

GET 2 FREE BOOKS!

CLAIM NOW!
Return this card today to get 2 FREE Books and 2 FREE Bonus Gifts!

YES! Please send me the **2 FREE books** and **2 FREE gifts** for which I qualify. I understand that I am under no obligation to purchase anything further, as explained on the back of this card.

▼ DETACH AND MAIL CARD TODAY!

PLACE FREE GIFTS SEAL HERE

❏ I prefer the regular-print edition
105/305 IDL GKCD

❏ I prefer the larger-print edition
122/322 IDL GKCD

FIRST NAME

LAST NAME

ADDRESS

APT.#

CITY

STATE/PROV.

ZIP/POSTAL CODE

LI-516-IVH16

If offer card is missing write to: Reader Service, P.O. Box 1867, Buffalo, NY 14240-1867 or visit www.ReaderService.com ▼

BUSINESS REPLY MAIL
FIRST-CLASS MAIL   PERMIT NO. 717   BUFFALO, NY

POSTAGE WILL BE PAID BY ADDRESSEE

READER SERVICE
PO BOX 1867
BUFFALO NY 14240-9952

NO POSTAGE
NECESSARY
IF MAILED
IN THE
UNITED STATES

where. Friday night you barely touched on our demands. I wanted to see you shake a fist and challenge the voters. Point out the prejudice they hold against us."

"You think that would win voters?"

"What I think is that you're forgetting why you were chosen to represent us." He wagged a finger at her. "Not that *I* chose you. You're too young. Too inexperienced. Too naive."

His face flushing, Gideon grabbed her upper arms and roughly shook her. Almost unbalancing her. Then, with a surprised wheeze of protest, his own arms were grasped and he was spun around to face a grim Grady Hunter.

"Keep your hands to yourself, Mr. Edlow. Or I'll stand as a witness for Ms. Carston if she wants to file attempted assault charges."

"Stay out of this, Hunter," Gideon sputtered. "This is none of your business."

"When you laid a hand on her, you made it my business."

Gideon's fists clenched, and for a horrified moment, Sunshine feared he'd take a swing at Grady. But with a glare in her direction, he stepped back. "You and your Boy Scout here think this is over, Sunshine. But it's not. You aren't fit to represent our arts community in public office and you're not fit to run the Co-op."

With a murderous scowl in Grady's direction, he charged back across the street in the direction from which he'd come.

"Are you okay?"

From the stunned look on her face, she wasn't. But that revealing expression was immediately replaced by one of annoyance.

"You shouldn't have interfered, Grady." Her words

came softly, yet firmly. "I was handling the situation just fine."

She was mad at *him*?

"He grabbed you, Sunshine. He was shaking you."

"He wasn't hurting me. He was venting. He's not a happy man. Never has been. And he's always resented the fact that I was hired to manage the Co-op rather than him."

"You didn't feel threatened when he grabbed you? Your face told another story."

"He startled me. That's all." She cast a regretful look in the direction in which Gideon had disappeared. "I wish you hadn't interfered. It'll make things harder for me."

"Excuse me? I don't think it's acceptable for a man to shake a woman like that." He studied her. "Do you?"

For a moment he thought she wasn't going to answer. Then, almost reluctantly, she responded. "No. But at times my ex-husband could get a little...physical."

Something inside Grady jolted.

"Not that he ever hurt," she quickly added. "But like Gideon, he had a temper."

"I have a temper, too, but you don't see me shaking women until their teeth rattle."

She motioned impatiently. "Look, Grady, I don't want to discuss this. My ex is out of my life. It's in the past. So let's let it drop."

She started to move around him, but he sidestepped to block her way. "Not just yet. Your ex-husband may be long gone, but Gideon is in the here and now. What did you mean my 'interfering' will make things harder on you?"

"I'll not discuss my personal life on a street corner." She gave him a pointed look, then flashed a bright smile to a woman with a toddler passing by them.

He motioned to the open door of the Hunter store. "Is that private enough? The contractor and his crew knocked off at noon today."

With an exasperated sigh, she preceded him into the shadowed interior. He closed the glass-paned door behind them, but she moved farther into the building, taking in the renovated space. He watched in silence.

Eventually she looked back at him. "Wow. The exposed brick and refinished woodwork are amazing."

It did look good. Ted and his crew had outdone themselves in giving him what he'd envisioned. Display cases would be delivered next week. He'd gone out on a limb to have enlargements made of some of his own wildlife photos. Framing would be completed before the mid-month grand opening. No, they wouldn't be for sale, but somehow the thought of putting them on the wall here— instead of a stranger's work purchased off the internet— gave him a deep sense of satisfaction.

But he wasn't letting Sunshine off the hook.

"How is it that my stepping in when Gideon was out of line going to make things harder for you?"

She looked away from him, moving to where she could run her fingertips along the polished surface of wood shelving. "You have to understand, Grady, that Gideon is a force to be reckoned with."

"Or at least he *thinks* he is." Gideon's bluster didn't faze him.

"When the Hunter Ridge Artists' Cooperative was getting off the ground, the members of the fledgling organization hired me. Gideon had wanted the position for himself but, for obvious reasons, the membership felt neither his personality nor his experience were suitably matched. He resented that. Resents me."

"So he's made it rough on you from the beginning."

"He and a couple of others who look up to him. For each step forward that I attempt to take, they push back. Fortunately, I have the full support of the majority of the membership, including our officers, but dealing with Gideon has never been pleasant."

"From what I overheard, he has a chip on his shoulder. But that's no excuse for grabbing you like he did."

"No, but I'm fine. Unhurt. His outbursts are nothing new."

"No? So what do you think he was driving at when he said this isn't over and that you're unfit to run the Co-op or run for office? That sounds like a veiled threat to me."

"I won't pretend to understand Gideon's thinking. But knowing him, he'll attempt to further slander me at the weekly Co-op meetings. Behind the scenes he'll try to win more members in whatever way he can to force me out."

"Isn't that illegal?"

"He's never been shy in letting me know that he wants to unseat me from managing the Co-op. I think the membership asking me to represent them on the town council was the last straw."

He leaned against an oak checkout counter, arms folded. "I don't like this one bit."

"I appreciate your concern but—no offense intended—like Gideon said, this is none of your business. I'd appreciate it if you'd stay out of it in the future."

Why was she so determined to make light of that jerk's behavior and chastise *him* for stepping in?

"You need to promise me that you won't meet with him anywhere except in a public place. Don't let him get you alone, not even corner you by yourself at a meeting where he could let his temper fly without any witnesses."

"I can't make that promise, but I assure you I'll be on my guard."

He raised his hands in surrender, irritation coloring his tone. "Pardon me for jumping in where I'm not wanted."

"Grady, don't be like that. I appreciate your concern. And thank you for wanting to protect me. But truly, your intervention will make him more determined to get me fired. I can't afford to lose this job. I have Tessa to support."

"I'm sorry if you think my stepping in added fuel to the fire. But in my opinion, he's a powder keg waiting to go off and his behavior needs to be nipped in the bud." Easy enough for him to say, though. He wasn't a single mother who needed a job to keep a roof over her daughter's head and food on the table. "I understand where you're coming from, Sunshine. Honestly, I do. But don't allow this guy to bully you. If he does it again, promise me you'll go to the authorities. I'm seriously thinking about doing that myself."

"Please, Grady, don't do that."

"Then, you'll promise me that if he approaches you again, tries to intimidate you, you'll report him?"

Warring emotions flashed through her eyes. Irritation. Resentment. And finally—relief? When she nodded, he could barely keep himself from reaching for her. To hug her for making that concession.

For a long moment their gazes held, then abruptly she glanced at her watch. "Look, I've got to run. Benton's covering for me at the gallery so I can do a few errands."

She moved briskly to the door and opened it.

"We're still on for tonight?" he called out. This would be their final review of the presentation. Their last evening together. He'd hit the grocery store last night, picking up cheesecake, potatoes to bake and filet mignon to grill.

A thank-you gift.

Hand on the doorknob, she paused to look at him, her expression suddenly apologetic. "I'm sorry, something's come up and I have to cancel. But I'll email the presentation to you. I think we're basically done if you think it's good to go. Take a look at it and let me know."

With a fleeting smile, she was gone.

Something had come up?

Grady groaned. He'd obviously overstepped his bounds when he'd instinctively stepped in to halt Gideon, the macho-minded rescue somehow sinking his ship.

And what ship might that be, Grady? Winning a lady's heart?

He kicked aside the betraying thought. He had absolutely no designs on Sunshine Carston. None.

Right?

Chapter Eleven

"You're coming to the Hideaway Saturday evening, aren't you, Sunshine?" Delaney Marks Hunter, her wavy, sun-streaked blond hair tumbling around her shoulders, paused at the bottom of the Co-op gallery staircase that led not only to Sunshine's apartment, but to several small studios where Delaney had started taking silversmithing lessons from Benton Mason during the summer.

Sunshine had received and responded to the invitation Delaney was referring to with mixed emotions. Elaine and Dave Hunter were hosting a gathering of current town council members, candidates and other prominent people in the community. It was hard to imagine socializing with Irvin after his ungallant performance a week ago, but that was not what bothered her most.

"I'll be there. My friend Tori is going watch Tessa."

"Bring Tessa along. Tori, too." Delaney's smile broadened, obviously thrilled to be a Hunter now. Having married into the family a month ago, she was already comfortable speaking on their behalf. "The Hunters would be fine with that."

"I think a night of boring local politics might be a bit much for both."

"Our kids will be there. At least for the cookout." Luke had three children, which Delaney already thought of as her own and had earlier confided her intent to adopt. "Claire—one of Luke's twin sisters—and her kids are in town to help out, so they'll be there, too. And I imagine several others will bring their children. The Hunters are all about family. You should see Grady when he's surrounded by his nieces and nephews. He's going to make a great dad some day."

He'd certainly won Tessa's heart.

The invitation had been addressed to Sunshine Carston and family, noting she could bring a guest. But with Tori busy researching how the Hunters may have swindled Sunshine's great-great-grandparents out of their property, she'd likely balk at being asked to socialize with them. And although Tessa might enjoy playing with the other kids, her obsession with Grady being her hero didn't need to be fueled further. When Tessa had spied him at church last Sunday, she'd gone running with arms outstretched to the poor surprised man. Recovering, he'd laughed, picked her up and lifted her high before setting her back on her feet. Not good.

"It's nice of the Hunters to plan something like this." Even though it was awkward. Not only was she hoping to prove their ancestor had done hers wrong, but she'd been nagged by guilt for days at having let Grady down Tuesday night—and having put him off on Thursday, as well. But after Gideon's accusations about her "getting cozy" with Grady, she'd had no choice.

She had a fine line to walk, keeping the two factions of the Co-op on speaking terms and unified in purpose. While Gideon had kept a physical distance at Wednesday evening's meeting—no doubt wary after having been confronted by Grady—he'd challenged her again and again.

She could *not* lose her job and the apartment that came with it. Maybe at tonight's veterans-hosted dinner she'd have the opportunity to clarify things with Grady. To smooth the gulf between them that she'd been forced to create.

"Well, I'll see you then!" Always full of energy, Delaney dashed up the stairs.

Over the next several hours, Sunshine waited on customers at the gallery, then got cleaned up and changed clothes for the evening's event. Would Irvin be on better behavior tonight?

The sun had set by the time she arrived at the Log Cabin Café, owner and former marine William "Packy" Westin welcoming her to a spacious back room where others were gathering for an opportunity to get to know the candidates. She'd expected mostly males, but spouses, dates and female vets were also in attendance.

A burly guy in his early sixties with a close-cropped beard, Packy's shaved head shone under the overhead lights as he helped her remove her coat and led her to her seat at the front of a U-shaped table arrangement.

Next to Grady, thankfully, and not Irvin.

Her breath caught unexpectedly as Grady's warm gaze met hers without a trace of the distancing between them that she'd feared.

"Beautiful dress, Sunshine."

Heat warmed her cheeks. Tori had loaned it to her. A black sheath that skimmed her figure, topped by a fitted ruby sweater jacket. Strappy high heels gave it an added touch of style that she didn't often indulge in. And to think she'd almost resorted to wool slacks, turtleneck and flats because the evening had turned nippy.

Now, seeing that appreciative spark in Grady's eyes, she knew she'd made the right choice.

With Packy on one side of her and Grady on the other, the meal passed pleasantly, not allowing her much time to notice the butterflies in her stomach. Then, much to her relief, Irvin was called upon to present first, then her and finally Grady.

All that worry of Irvin putting on a repeat performance at her expense had been for nothing. This group asked harder questions of Mr. Baydlin than the others had, politely but pointedly putting him on the spot a few times. That let a little of the hot air out of him. With former army vet and fellow artist Benton Mason and his wife in attendance, she more confidently presented her hopes that the old and new could work together to improve the economy for Hunter Ridge.

The evening was unexpectedly painless and, following some mingling and answering questions one-on-one, by nine thirty the guests began to disperse. She'd done it. Made it through another event. If only the remaining ones would be so effortless.

Among the last to leave, Grady held out her coat and helped her to slip it on. "May I walk you to your car?"

"If you don't mind. I parked out back and the lighting isn't that good."

"My pleasure."

Attempting to tamp down the rapid beating of her heart, she followed Grady down a short hallway. Then he held open the door and they stepped out into the night.

"Brrr." She pulled her coat collar up around her neck, wishing she'd brought along her wool scarf and leather gloves. She took note of Grady's shirtsleeves. "Didn't you bring a coat?"

"It's inside. I'll get it after I see you to your car."

Carefully navigating the steps, Sunshine gave a silent sigh of relief when she reached the bottom without mishap, acutely conscious of Grady's hand grazing her waist at the back of her coat.

"Where are you parked?"

"Over there." She clicked a button on her car key, the SUV's taillights momentarily illuminating, but she immediately concentrated on negotiating the graveled parking lot with care. Not easy in high heels after dark.

They almost made it to her vehicle when her footing gave way. A pothole. With a startled cry, she fought to regain her balance, only to be caught by Grady. Steadied. Grateful, she turned to thank him.

But he was unexpectedly close.

Her breathing suddenly shallow, she stared up at him and in the dim light saw his eyes widen slightly, as surprised to find her in his arms as she was to be there.

"Grady—" Their gazes locked, and she could feel his heart beating where her hand rested on his shirtfront. But she couldn't voice the words of thanks that needed to be said. "I—"

He placed his finger gently to her lips to silence her.

Somewhere in the distance, as a barely there breeze touched her cheek, she could hear the cry of a night bird. The bark of a dog. The sound of muted laughter coming from one of the other restaurants along the main road through town.

And then, ever so slowly he closed his eyes and leaned forward until she could feel his soft breath inches from her lips.

He is going to kiss me. She should stop him. And yet… her own eyes closed and her lips parted in anticipation.

"Grady!" Packy's marine-tough voice barreled across the darkened parking lot.

They jerked apart. Staring at each other as if dazed.

"You out there, Grady?" Packy remained silhouetted at the restaurant's back door.

"Yeah." Grady cleared his throat, then raised his voice. "Yeah, I'm here, Packy."

"You left your jacket. Don't forget to come back and get it."

"Will do."

Packy disappeared from the doorway and they were again alone. But the moment had been broken.

Grady again cleared his throat. "I guess I'd better let you get in your vehicle and get warmed up."

From the second he'd taken her into his arms, however, she'd no longer been aware of the cold but had been flooded by a curious warmth. A warmth that now quickly ebbed. With a shiver, she took the final steps to her SUV, where she unlocked the door. He held it open as she seated herself, the glare of the interior light further stripping away the fleeting thrill of what had happened.

What had *almost* happened.

"Good night, Sunshine." Grady's tone was flat, impersonal, as he shut the door, then stepped back into the shadows.

Now trembling, Sunshine started the engine, then carefully backed out and exited the almost empty parking lot.

Once on the road to home, she pressed her unsteady fingers lightly to her lips.

"Either grab a box and help, Grady, or get out of the way." Luke, arms laden with an oversize plastic bin, elbowed his way past him and onto the patio at the back of the inn.

With a midafternoon wind kicking up, they'd delayed patio preparation until the last minute. Mom hadn't wanted to risk everything getting blown into the next county. But now, with the sun dipping below the towering treetops, calm had returned. Time for all hands on deck.

"Are you feeling all right, Grady?" Grandma Jo looking at him with concern, lifted her hand to his forehead. "No fever. But you haven't been yourself today."

Luke rolled his eyes at him as, bin delivered, he returned to the inn.

"Stuff on my mind I guess, Grandma."

She studied him with open curiosity, then, without further comment, returned inside.

He had a lot on his mind, all right. Like the fact that not only had he almost kissed Sunshine last night, but she'd be arriving any minute. What would he say to her? Should he pretend nothing happened between them at all? Apologize?

Heading into the inn, he grabbed one of the bins out of the storage room and carried it outside to where Rio was unpacking others in front of the big outdoor fireplace. Plastic table covers. Salt and pepper shakers. Cloth napkins.

"Need any help there?" he felt obligated to ask.

She looked up at him. "Thanks, but I think I've got it. You could finish setting up tables for the kids, though, and tell Luke to bring out the rest of the folding chairs. We're expecting about fifty. That's including maybe a dozen children."

Fifty. With that many packed out here, he might not have to worry too much about interacting with Sunshine after all. Besides, as a candidate for town council she'd have her focus on meeting people, making a good impression, baby kissing and all that.

Inwardly he groaned. Why did he have to think of *kissing*?

But instantly his thoughts flew to the dark parking lot behind the Log Cabin Café. Would he ever be back there again without thinking of last night? When he'd kept Sunshine from falling, she'd turned in his arms and... his mind had converted to mush. If Packy hadn't hollered out the door, well, he'd be in a bigger heap of trouble than he was right now.

"Grady?"

He jerked back to the present where Rio was staring up at him doubtfully.

"Are you going to stand there or are you going to deliver my message to Luke and get the tables set up?"

"On it."

He had to get his head out of the clouds. Fast.

"There you are!" His sister Claire, one of the twins, caught his arm just as he stepped inside to search for Luke. "I've been back home for a week and have hardly seen you."

She gave him a hug. She was so different from their youngest sister, Rio, who was a loner who'd far prefer to spend her time out in the stable with the horses than deal with a crowd of people. Which meant that after her duties here were completed, she'd pull a disappearing act.

Not Claire, though. She loved being in the thick of things, would thrive on playing hostess at Hunter's Hideaway even if only during a visit. Since marrying and moving to Dallas, she didn't often get back once she and Del had three kids aged five and under.

"I've been around." He lowered his voice. "Mom sure appreciates your coming back to help right now. We all do."

"Flying in and out solo for Luke and Delaney's wedding reminded me how much I miss you all. Del's out of the country on business for a few weeks, so I saw no reason why I shouldn't pack up the kids and come on home to help out. Nothing to stop me."

"So," he continued, "do you think Mom's up to this tonight? When she announced her intentions on Sunday not to cancel the barbecue, you could have knocked me over with a feather."

"I imagine having something other than chemo treatments to look forward to perked her up this week. I know she looked tired when I got here, but don't you think she's seemed livelier the past few days?"

"Maybe. I don't want her overdoing it, though. And her possibly being exposed to colds or flu with all these kids running around concerns me, but she wouldn't hear of asking guests not to bring their children. I don't much care, either, that she's giving her opponents ammunition to use against her if she isn't up to par tonight."

Irv's earlier potshots still rankled.

Claire frowned. "Do you think Irvin and that Sunshine woman would do that? I don't put it past Irv, of course. He was in Dad's high school graduating class and Dad's never cared for him. But I don't know much about this Carston lady. She's lived here a couple of years, right? What do you know about her?"

Warmth crept up his neck.

What did he know about Sunshine? Well, she was a good mother. A hard worker. A fine artist. She knew a lot about marketing, which she'd been willing to share with him. Stubborn at times, but she had a smile that invariably coaxed out one of his own.

"I only recently met her, so I couldn't say." Claire didn't need to know how close he'd come to kissing her. "But I don't think she'd take advantage. I was thinking more of Baydlin. You know I'm filling in for Mom at election-related events, right? She'd hardly started chemo when he was raising questions about her fitness for office."

He glanced back through the door to the patio, noting that while he'd stood there jawing with Claire, a surprising number of guests had arrived, mingling as Dad fired up the gas grills.

"Hey, sis." He touched her arm. "Could you find Luke for me? Rio needs him to bring out more folding chairs. I'm supposed to be setting up tables for the kids."

"Sure." Then she leaned close, her eyes twinkling and voice lowered conspiratorially. "Let's have lunch sometime next week, okay? You need to catch me up on your love life."

He laughed. "That shouldn't take long."

"No one special yet, Grady?" She eyed him with concern and, once again, heat stole up his neck. "I know Jasmine left a bad taste in your mouth, but don't give up hope. We serve a big God. It can happen when you least expect it."

"Don't think I'll hold my breath."

She made a pouty face. "You're a wonderful man, and you deserve a wonderful woman. It's a matter of time. One of these days you're going to turn around and, when you least expect it, there she'll be."

She gave him a hug, then headed off.

He stood there a moment longer, contemplating Claire's ever-optimistic words. Then he pushed open the door and stepped out onto the patio—just as Sunshine rounded the corner of the inn.

Chapter Twelve

Sunshine's breath caught as she looked across the crowded patio—and right into Grady Hunter's eyes.

More handsome than ever, he stood looking at her with an intensity every bit as potent as what she remembered from last night. Despite the many times she'd replayed those moments in her mind, wondering if it might have been a dream, maybe she hadn't made it up?

Which meant it was all the more important to steer clear of him this evening. She'd given it considerable thought—and prayer—and concluded she had no business falling for a Hunter. Her history and that of his family were too intermingled, went too far back. When the time came that she could finally prove her suspicions against Grady's ancestors, she didn't want a romantic entanglement holding her back from claiming what rightfully belonged to her and her daughter.

With considerable effort, she broke eye contact and strode purposefully into the midst of the gathering just as Elaine Hunter joined her guests. For a moment Sunshine thought she'd restyled her sandy-brown, previously shoulder-length hair, then immediately realized the sassy new cut was a wig. She'd heard a few days ago that not too long into chemo, Elaine had courageously had her head shaved in anticipation of losing her hair. She'd started chemo barely a month ago and had lost weight. Nothing drastic, but the fullness had left her face. She was looking better, though, than Sunshine would have expected from what Grady had told her about how sick his mother had been.

This image of a still somewhat plucky Elaine should dispel any hopes Irvin Baydlin had of discrediting her with voters.

But before Sunshine could make her way through the crowd to thank her hostess for the invitation, Irvin suddenly appeared at Elaine's side. Obviously fawning over her from the looks of it. But surely he didn't believe Grady hadn't shared the snide remarks he'd made about her at the parent-teacher meeting. Then again, maybe Grady hadn't, for fear of distressing his mother and Irvin was betting on that.

Looking around for other familiar faces, she spied Delaney talking to an older woman—Josephine Hunter—and edged her way in their direction.

Delaney's smile brightened as she saw her. "Grandma Jo, have you met Sunshine Carston?" She quickly made introductions.

"I'm delighted you could join us this evening, Sunshine," the older woman acknowledged. "It's long been a family tradition to gather town council candidates for a relaxing, nonpolitically focused evening. A chance to get to know one another and each other's families on an informal basis."

Was that no-politicking comment intended as a reminder to a newcomer who'd barged her way into the town's affairs?

"I appreciate the invitation." Although she attempted

to stay focused on the immediate conversation, her radar couldn't help but note Grady moving among the guests, heading to where Mr. Baydlin remained glued to Elaine's side.

A protector by nature. That was Grady through and through.

Her stomach fluttered as again she recalled how he'd prevented her from falling last night. Held her gently but securely. And when she'd looked up at him…

"I understand you have a daughter, Sunshine. A kindergartner?"

"Yes. Tessa."

"She's a sweetie," Delaney chimed in. "Black hair and big brown eyes."

Ah, good. Grady had reached his mother's side and Irvin was slinking off. But she didn't much care for the smugly satisfied look on her fellow candidate's face. No doubt he'd been pumping Elaine under the guise of concern for her health.

With the mouthwatering scent of grilled meats and vegetables now filling the early-evening air, she chatted with Delaney and Mrs. Hunter awhile longer, then introduced herself to others she didn't know, including several of Grady's family members. It was nice, however, not to be expected to discuss the upcoming election. She hadn't realized how stressful that had become this past month, feeling pressured to somehow steer the topic to her campaign and solicit feedback from potential voters.

Across the way she again saw Grady, surrounded by a group of jabbering kids as he set up card tables and his brother, Luke, brought in folding chairs. She recognized Luke and Delaney's eight-year-old daughter, Chloe. But were any of the other children Grady's nieces and nephews? One laughing little fellow, about two years old, was lifted high into the air and settled on the big man's broad shoulders. Naturally, that set off a chorus of "Do me! Do me!"

From across the patio, his gaze was drawn to hers. But her smile hadn't even reached her lips before he looked away to give the youngsters his full attention.

As the sun dipped farther behind the towering ponderosas, adults and children lined up at a long, makeshift buffet to fill plates with hamburgers, hot dogs and veggie burgers. Potato salad. Baked beans. Cheesy potatoes. And more.

Now cast in shade, the patio was considerably cooler, although nowhere near the chill of the previous night. A fire crackled in the big stone outdoor fireplace and the strategically placed propane patio heaters were lit, offering warmth and a cozy glow, as well. Nevertheless, she was glad to have brought along a jacket.

Plate filled with food, she scanned the surrounding tables, looking for a place to sit. She'd hardly taken a step when Grady, a piled-high plate gripped in his hands, appeared at her side.

"I need to speak to you."

Please don't let him bring up last night.

But his expression gave nothing away. "Um, sure."

He nodded to one of the empty tables, then led the way. When they were seated, he poured them both a glass of iced tea and spread a napkin across his lap. Then he leaned toward her, his tone, to her relief, all business.

"I thought you should know that Mom said Irvin was trying to pin down her opinion of you."

"Why would he do that?"

"He probably figured Mom knows you better than he does, that she might shed light on something juicy he could use against you in the campaign."

She crumpled inside. "So your mother—?"

"Was on to him immediately and deflected his not-so-subtle inquiries. But she thought you should know, seeing as how he'd unfairly targeted you at the parent-teacher meeting."

She glanced across the patio to where Grady's mother and father sat, deep in conversation with those at their table. She wouldn't have expected Elaine, her opponent, to thwart Irvin on her behalf, let alone warn her of his intentions.

"Please thank your mother for me, will you?"

"I will." Then he motioned almost self-consciously to their plates. "Food's getting cold."

For an excruciatingly long span of time they ate in silence. Side by side, elbows mere inches from each other, he was acutely aware of the petite woman seated next to him. Her sweet scent. Her graceful movements as she reached for her tea glass. The way she occasionally paused to lift her cloth napkin to her lips…

He drew in a deep breath. He wasn't often at a loss for words, but his mind roamed unsuccessfully for a topic of conversation. Maybe it hadn't been a good idea to sit down together. Had his family noticed them sitting off by themselves? Irv?

He shifted uncomfortably in his chair, suddenly feeling as if all eyes were on them.

"What did you think of the presentation I put together, Grady?"

Her soft words startled him but, relieved, he gratefully responded. "I'm ashamed to admit I haven't had a single minute to look at it. Another project took precedence."

Disappointment clouded her eyes. Had his seeming indifference to her work hurt her?

"I've been up to my eyeballs," he said quickly, "in preparations for the grand opening two weeks from today. You know the old Murphy's Law? Well, multiply that times ten this past week."

"I'm sorry to hear that."

"Yeah, it's been wild. A delay in a number of deliveries. The guy who designed the website had problems with the host server. And there were unexpected issues with obtaining final approval paperwork. But—" He managed a smile, hoping he'd convinced her that he hadn't put off reviewing her presentation because he considered it of no value. "After Herculean effort on the part of those involved, everything's been resolved. Things should settle down next week."

"Good."

Once again they lapsed into silence. Resumed eating.

This was ridiculous. Maybe he was stuck-up for thinking her thoughts were gravitating back to last night as did his. But this couldn't go on. Abruptly he pushed back his empty plate and downed the remainder of his tea. Then he clasped his hands on the table in front of him and pinned her with a determined look.

"Okay, let's stop tiptoeing around each other and get this out in the open."

Startled eyes met his, her face flushing.

"I think we both know that something happened between us last night. Or rather, almost happened. And it's built a barrier that can't be allowed to remain since we'll be seeing each other on a regular basis at political events."

After a moment's hesitation, she placed her fork on her half-eaten plate and settled her hands in her lap. Despite her wary gaze, a faint smile touched her lips. "From the looks of your mother tonight, your stand-in duties may be a thing of the past."

"Don't let appearances fool you. It's been several days since her last chemo treatment and today she spent most of her time in bed, resting up for tonight." He tipped a look of mild reprimand in her direction. "And don't try to change the subject. I think I wouldn't be speaking out of line if I said that there's an…attraction. You know, between us. And it came to a head last night. Would you agree?"

For a moment he thought she'd deny it, but then she nodded.

"I like you, Sunshine. I'm under the impression you think I'm okay, too." His eyes searched hers, but she only stared back at him, her feelings masked. "I may be mistaken, but I don't think either of us is looking for a relationship right now."

"I—" She paused. "That's correct."

He relaxed only slightly, disturbed that her confirmation didn't shoot off any fireworks of relief. "Please don't take my reluctance to get involved right now the wrong way. As I said, I like you. You're a beautiful, bright young woman. But it's tricky dating a woman with a kid. I don't make a habit of it."

She gave a brittle laugh. "You make it sound as though involvement with someone's child is something undesirable. That surprises me. I was under the impression you like children."

"I do. And that's exactly why I'm careful about who I date. I don't want to hurt a kid when things don't work out between the adults."

"Is that experience talking?"

"Unfortunately, yes."

"Well, don't lose any sleep over sharing that with me. I don't take it personally. To be honest, the last thing I need right now is another romantic entanglement."

"Because of your ex? From what you've told me, it doesn't sound like you should spend too much time mourning the loss of him."

"He's very talented—a musician in a country band. He has a great sense of humor. Works hard. Charms the socks off the ladies. Like you in those respects."

That comparison left a sour taste in his mouth. "So if he was such a great guy, what happened?"

She stared across the patio for a long moment, the flicker of light from a table candle illuminating the softness of her face. Her troubled eyes. "We were young. Or at least I was. He's nine years my senior. You know, one of those classic little-girl-without-a-strong-male-role-model-goes-looking-for-one scenarios."

"Not surprising."

She shrugged. "Anyway, we got married when I was nineteen. And things were good for several years. It was exciting traveling with him and his band. They were popular throughout the Southwest, with Nashville-bound stars in their eyes. But then…" She quirked a smile. "Pregnancy."

"He wasn't happy about that?"

"At first he was. But once Tessa was born, it became harder and harder for me to be on the road. To help with the driving, the set up and breakdown. The kid stuff I had to drag along irritated him. And the diapers. A baby crying when he was trying to sleep. No longer having me at his beck and call."

"Sounds like a selfish jerk."

"Sometimes. But he was a man with dreams—ones that didn't include hauling around a diaper bag. He wanted me to leave Tessa with my mom." Her voice drifted off, then came back strong. "Don't get me wrong. I love my mother, but she could be hard to please. I grew up with a cloud of disapproval hanging over my head, so there was no way I was going to leave the offspring of a man she'd warned me about in her care for long stretches of time. I did everything I could, though, to make things work, to stay on the road with him. But it wasn't enough and he said adios."

"Does he keep in contact with you? With his daughter?"

"Are you kidding? The band continues to struggle. They live out of cheap hotels and campers on the back of their trucks. I expect to hear anytime now that they've broken up, gone their separate ways. With only sporadic paychecks, of course, there's rarely a child-support payment. Nor does Jerrel Carston want any part in Tessa's life. Or mine."

Grady's hand clenched, resisting reaching down to take Sunshine's in his. It was that tenderhearted thinking last night that had got them where they were now. Confessing they weren't ready for a relationship.

"So you see," Sunshine said almost brightly, "why I neither take offense that you're cautious about involvement with some woman's kid, nor am I hurt by your honesty about your feelings about me. We're on the same page."

"So we're good?"

"We're good."

Then, why doesn't it feel good?

She glanced at her surroundings, where others had finished their meal and were moving from table to table to greet fellow guests. "I guess I'd better get out and mingle."

"I should do the same. Show a little Hunter hospitality. And maybe I'll grab a bowlful of that ice cream I see they're serving now."

"I want to slip over there to personally thank your mother for inviting me. And meet your father."

When she stood, he rose, too, oddly dissatisfied with the way their conversation was ending. He lightly touched her arm. "Hey, when you're ready to leave, find me okay? I'll walk you to your car."

Catching the deliberately teasing lilt in this tone, she laughed. "Thank you, but I'll pass on your gentlemanly offer this time, Mr. Hunter. I've come prepared for a trek across your graveled parking lot." She patted her jacket pocket. "Flashlight and—" she lifted her loafer-clad foot and wiggled it "—no heels."

They stood smiling at each other, neither making any attempt to hurry off to their social obligations.

Grady silently absorbed the loveliness of the woman before him. Was he being stupid about his unwillingness to get involved with a woman who had a child? Using it as an excuse not to risk loving again? But no matter what conclusions he came to on that issue, she'd been clear enough tonight that she wasn't ready for another relationship.

As if suddenly self-conscious under his thoughtful gaze, the laughter faded from Sunshine's eyes. She lifted her hand in a parting wave, leaving Grady with an inexplicable ache in the region of his heart.

Chapter Thirteen

"I'm praying everything will work out the way you want it to, Tori." Sunshine stood just inside the guest room doorway watching as her friend packed her suitcase late Saturday afternoon. Her fiancé had called a short while ago and wanted her to come back to Jerome, saying they needed to talk.

Which left Sunshine with a real bad feeling. If a man had decided in favor of reconfirming his engagement, wouldn't he show up on his fiancée's doorstep, not ask her to drive over three hours to see him?

"That's just it." Tori tucked her hair dryer into a side pocket. "I'm no longer sure how I want it to work out."

"Your feelings toward Heath have changed? Absence isn't making the heart grow fonder?"

"I love him with all my heart, but I don't want to be his choice by default because nothing better came along during our separation." Tori checked the contents of her bag, then zipped it shut. "Guess I'd better hit the road. I'll come back and get the rest of my stuff, you know, if—"

Impulsively, Sunshine gave her friend a quick hug. "No matter what, everything is going to be okay. If

Heath's stupid enough to let you go, God has something better in mind."

"I keep telling myself that." She lifted her bag from the bed. "I'll call you, whatever the outcome. And thanks for letting me stay here. Tessa has been such a wonderful distraction. You're fortunate to have her. I only wish…"

Tori shook her head with regret, as if deciding her hopes were better left unshared.

"Wish what?"

"That God would bring a special man into your life. Someone like Grady Hunter. You know, real hero material."

A prick of sadness pierced Sunshine's heart, an echo of the melancholy that had lingered since her encounter with Grady a week ago.

He might be genuine hero material, but he wasn't looking for a woman with a child. He'd said he didn't want to risk hurting a kid, but maybe, as with Jerrel, the real issue was that a kid took time and attention. Attention away from him. Even if she pulled out of the campaign and dropped the pursuit of proof that would hold his family accountable for wrongs done to hers, there would be no future there. He'd made that clear last weekend.

"It will be dark before long," Sunshine reminded as Tori departed. "Call me when you get there so I know you made it safely."

Despite the comforting sound of Tessa chatting with her dolls, the apartment seemed unbearably empty once Tori departed. Maybe she'd fix them something simple for supper, then pop in a Disney DVD to watch together. Or maybe…?

"Tessa?" She stepped to the open doorway of her daughter's room, her heart, as always, warming at the sight of the child God had given her. "How would you like to have supper at the Log Cabin Café tonight?"

With money tight, they didn't eat out often, but she had a coupon. Maybe they could split the Saturday-night burger special.

Tessa's face lit up. She loved Packy, who always brought her a special treat on the rare excursions to his restaurant. A small cup of yogurt or a piece of candy. "Can we have sweet potato fries?"

"I see no reason why not."

Tessa scrambled to her feet. "Are we going now?"

"It's a little early. I'll come get you when we're ready to go." Restless and highly conscious of Tori's departure to a future that might be decided tonight, Sunshine wandered to the kitchen and began straightening the pantry. There was nothing, in her opinion, like getting organized to chase away the blues. But she'd barely gotten started when Tori's words resurfaced in her mind.

I wish God would bring a special man into your life.

Sunshine sighed. Well, He hadn't. Maybe He never would. But the Bible said God had a good plan for her. A plan not to bring harm, but to give her a hope and a future. She had to hang on tight to that now, just as she had since Jerrel had walked out of her life.

Someone like Grady Hunter.

She plopped a can of beans on the shelf with a thud. That door was closed, and there was no point in dwelling on it.

You know, real hero material.

Nonsense. She didn't need a hero. She and Tessa were doing fine on their own. Hadn't God generously given her a job that came with housing? A schedule that allowed her time to paint in order to supplement her income and spend quality time with Tessa? And hadn't He, too, brought any number of people into her life at exactly the right moment?

Like Tori, who'd stepped in to care for Tessa when Sunshine needed more time for campaigning. And someone to assist when her vehicle had conked out on the highway at night. To help get her SUV fixed. And to rescue Tessa when she'd gotten caught on the slide.

With a growl of irritation, Sunshine halted herself before she slammed another can onto the shelf. Just because Grady happened to fill a few of those roles, that didn't mean he was meant to be *her* hero. Or Tessa's.

He'd made it clear he wasn't interested in anything like that. But could she stand to live in this town if he someday became some other woman's hero?

"I admit it surprises me, but I actually like Sunshine." Across the table from Grady at the Log Cabin Café Saturday night, Luke took a final sip from his coffee mug. Then he smiled at his bride seated next to him in the high-backed booth. "Delaney said *she* did. But until last weekend, I didn't agree."

He slid a look in Grady's direction. One intended to make his younger brother squirm.

"I like her, too," Rio, next to Grady, chimed in.

Grady looked around at the packed restaurant, animated conversations swirling around him keeping the sound volume to a low roar. Typical Saturday night. Was there any hope he could sneak out of here to escape the direction this conversation had taken?

"So what do you think of her, Grady?" Luke wasn't about to let him off the hook. "The two of you seemed to have a lot to talk about at the cookout."

"You noticed that, too?" Delaney laughed and slipped her arm into the crook of her husband's. But she was looking at her brother-in-law. "Seemed very chummy to me."

A smiling Rio elbowed him. "Have anything you want to fill us in on, Grady?"

Remembering how he and Rio had mercilessly teased Luke about Delaney a few short months ago, the tables were now turned. He pushed his plate away, conscious of everyone's eyes on him.

"Sunshine and I were talking business."

Rio giggled. "Nice try, Grady. Tell us another one."

"Maybe the three of you have forgotten, but Sunshine Carston's is Mom's *opponent*."

Luke grimaced. "There is that drawback. And the fact that she's the primary spokesperson for an artists' contingent that won't shut up."

"Now, Luke," Delaney chided, "they do have good points. I mean, why were they turned down on having an art-in-the-park event? That makes no sense to me."

"Because, sweetheart," Luke said, patting her hand in a patronizing manner that would likely get him yelled at once they got home, "they intended to bring in outside vendors—like food trucks and others who would take away from local businesses and restaurants. Summer is a make-it-or-break-it deal for most people around here. Losing ground one weekend a month for three or four months could be a significant loss."

"Or it could be—" she nudged her husband, undaunted "—that the event would draw even more business to the locals. Put Hunter Ridge on the map."

Grady grinned. "Looks as if you have your work cut out for you, Luke. Delaney's starting to think like one of them."

To his relief, the owner of the café appeared at their

table before the topic could switch back to him and Sunshine.

"Anything else I can get you folks? More coffee? Water?"

"I think that's it, Packy." Grady patted his own flat but full stomach. "Great meal as always. Thanks."

"You're welcome. Have a good rest of your evening." Packy placed the bill on the table and moved on to the next.

Grady snatched up the slip of paper, but he'd barely risen to his feet and moved away from the booth when he felt a tug on his sleeve.

"Hi, Grady!" Tessa, smiling ear to ear, threw her arms around him as Sunshine walked up behind her. He returned the exuberant hug.

"I'm sorry for the interruption." Sunshine looked apologetically at him and the others at the table. "But Tessa didn't want to leave without saying hello."

"Good to see you again." Luke nodded to Sunshine as he, too, slipped out of the booth. "I don't believe I've met your daughter."

Grady made introductions to his family, self-conscious as the little girl clung to his hand.

Tessa looked up at him, her expression reflecting awe. "You have a big family, don't you, Grady?"

"Yeah, and there are more who aren't here." As an only child, she probably found siblings a fascinating concept. "I have one brother and three sisters."

"Wow."

"Come on, Tessa. Time to go." Sunshine held out her hand.

"Can Grady walk home with us? It's dark outside."

Noting her voice was tinged with apprehension, he exchanged a quick glance with Sunshine. Was this what she'd alluded to earlier? Anxiety related to the mysterious presence in the little girl's closet?

"We'll be fine walking home, honey. There's nothing to be afraid of."

While Saturday night in town usually had lots of people out and about and they'd be safe on the way to their apartment, the gallant thing to do would be to see them safely home. But after that too-close-for-comfort incident in the parking lot last weekend, he sensed her reluctance.

As he quickly debated with himself, his family filed past him, Luke snagging the bill from his fingers.

"I'll get this. And Rio can ride home with us."

Looked as if that settled it. "I'd be happy to see you home, Tessa, if your mother doesn't mind my company."

"You don't mind, do you, Mommy?"

Tessa's eyes pleaded and, after a moment's indecision, Sunshine gave in. "Thank you, Grady."

But she wasn't happy about it.

Outside, she was relieved that the wind had died down and, although as chilly as a mid-October evening in the Arizona high country was expected to be, the walk would warm them.

She needn't have worried about making conversation. Gripping Grady's hand, Tessa chatted like a proverbial magpie, telling him about the late-season butterfly she'd seen at the park that morning, how her kindergarten teacher praised her for a picture she'd drawn and that Tori would be gone a few days.

Her daughter's enthusiasm at having this man's full attention again dredged up memories of her own childhood, triggering an ache in her heart for Tessa. Grady was right. When things didn't work out in relationships, innocent kids could get hurt. Although Grady barely hesitated when Tessa expressed hopes that he would accompany them, that concern had to have been on his mind.

As they neared the gallery door, Sunshine fished in her jacket pocket for the key, but she sensed Tessa slowing her pace, reluctant for the walk to come to an end.

"Mommy, can Grady come in and see my new goldfish?"

She should have anticipated this bedtime-delay tactic. "I imagine he's seen goldfish before."

"But he hasn't seen *my* goldfish." She looked up at him, her eyes imploring. "Please, Grady?"

He looked to Sunshine. "I have a few minutes. That is, if—"

"Okay. But we can't keep Grady long, honey. He has to walk back to the café and then drive home."

Tessa jumped up and down as Sunshine let them inside the gallery and locked the door behind them. Then Tessa eagerly pulled Grady forward, among the dimly illuminated displays and up the stairs to the apartment.

Acutely aware of Grady's presence beside her, Sunshine tensed as she inserted the key in the door.

Had she put away the stuffed animals Tessa had dragged to the living room that afternoon? Was the kitchen clean? And most of all, had Tori's research that she'd been reviewing before they left for the café been tucked out of sight?

As they stepped inside, she scanned the room. Everything appeared to be in order.

"Nice place." Grady's eyes took in their living quarters as Tessa again tugged him forward.

"My room is nice, too. Come and see."

At his questioning look, Sunshine nodded and he allowed Tessa to guide him into the diminutive space, softly lit by a bedside lamp. Big enough for a single bed, dresser and skirted nightstand, it had been decorated with secondhand and discount store finds that lent it a fashionable shabby-chic look. The white-painted furniture set off the pink floral bedspread, area rug and throw pillows. Dolls and stuffed animals lined a wall shelf next to the bed.

"There he is!" Tessa pointed proudly to the goldfish in a bowl atop her dresser. "Goldie."

Sunshine had bought the fish for her when in Canyon Springs on business earlier in the week, hoping the tiny fellow's presence might ease Tessa's nighttime fears. Unfortunately, Tessa insisted the aquatic creature was afraid of the dark and continued to keep the night-light on.

Grady leaned in to inspect her new friend. "That's a handsome-looking fish you have there."

"I know."

Then Tessa hurriedly rummaged through a dresser drawer.

Sunshine frowned. "What are you looking for, sweetheart?"

"My new jammies. The ones Tori bought me. I want Grady to see me in them." Locating them, she clutched them to her heart, a serious look on her face. "Don't leave, okay, Grady? I'll be right back."

"Tessa, I don't think—"

But Tessa wiggled past her and out the bedroom door. Seconds later, the bathroom door shut behind her.

"I'm sorry, Grady. She'll do about anything to avoid turning out the lights and being left in her room at bedtime. But I don't dare let her sleep with me and get that started."

"Don't be sorry. I'm not. She's a sweet kid."

But they both knew he didn't want to get attached to

a kid. At least not one that didn't belong to him or his family.

"I've seen quite a bit of activity next door this week." She moved to turn down Tessa's bed. Plumped a pillow. "So how are things going for the grand opening?"

She couldn't bring herself to ask him again if he'd looked at her presentation for his photography proposal, afraid it might not be what he'd hoped.

"Going good. Or as good as you can expect with it only a week away. The website is up and running and our team is processing orders."

"Wonderful."

Grady folded his arms. "So has there been any more talk of a petition to put us out of business?"

"Not to my knowledge."

"Gideon is keeping his distance?" Grady's eyes narrowed. "And his hands to himself?"

"He is." She didn't dare mention his rant at the last Co-op meeting.

"Here I am!" Dressed in her baby blue flannel and eyelet-trimmed nightwear, a beaming Tessa appeared in the doorway, arms outstretched like a miniature diva.

"Now, don't you look beautiful."

Tessa's smile broadened at Grady's praise. Then she stepped toward him and lifted her arm. "It's soft. See?"

His big hand brushed the delicate flannel sleeve. "Oh, wow, it is. I'm sure that keeps you warm, too."

"Uh-huh." She made a dive for her bed and scrambled to get herself situated. "You can tuck me in, Grady."

His surprised gaze met Sunshine's, searching hers for direction, permission. When she nodded, he sat on the edge of the bed, looking huge next to the tiny girl. After a moment's hesitation, he tucked the covers around her, then leaned in to place a kiss on her forehead.

Not unexpectedly, Tessa cast an apprehensive look around the room. "I forgot to close the closet door. Mommy?"

"I'll do it." For whatever reason, Tessa couldn't sleep without the door firmly closed and her night-light on. "But there's no reason to be afraid."

Tessa's hand crept out from under the covers to reach for Grady's hand and his big one swallowed up her tiny one. "So you're scared of something, are you, Tessa? Something that might come out of your closet?"

She nodded solemnly.

"I understand what it's like to be afraid."

"You do?"

"Sure. I've been scared lots of times."

"Mommy says there's nothing to be afraid of." Tessa darted a doubtful look in her direction.

"You know," Grady continued, his voice soothing, "there's nothing in that closet that can hurt you, don't you? Your mom wouldn't allow that and she wouldn't tell you there was nothing in there if there was. So you *know* there's nothing in there, right? But you *feel* scared anyway."

He ran a finger down the upper part of her flannel-clad arm. "And it's as if something has a hold of you right here, isn't it? Squeezing tight. And maybe your knees and your tummy hurt, too."

Tessa nodded again and he gently brushed her hair back from her face. "That's what I thought. But we both agree with your mom, right? Nothing is in the closet. So what I want you to do now is settle back on your pillow and close your eyes, okay?"

"'Kay."

But Tessa's eyes immediately flew open when he

turned off the bedside lamp, leaving the room illuminated only by the light coming through the bedroom door.

He gave her hand a squeeze. "Eyes closed, remember?"

Nodding again, she obeyed.

And then, in a low, gentle voice, he began to pray.

"Father God, Tessa is scared. She knows there's nothing in her closet, but it *feels* as if there is. As You know, feelings are powerful things. You gave them to us so we can enjoy the good things You give us and so they can warn us when there's danger. There's no danger here, but Tessa's feelings are mixed up and telling her there is."

Tears pricked Sunshine's eyes. This dear man, going before his Heavenly Father on her daughter's behalf. Understanding a little girl's fears. Not telling her, as Sunshine had repeatedly done, to stop being afraid.

"So we're here tonight asking in the name of Your son, Jesus," he continued, "that You grab hold of the feelings that are telling Tessa fibs. That You will make the scary things she's seeing in her mind go away. That You will make the feelings that are squeezing her body let go. Thank You."

Eyes still closed, Tessa nodded her agreement and once more Grady brushed back her hair, his voice gentle but firm. "Now, when bad feelings try to sneak in and start to squeeze you, I want you to say in your mind or out loud, 'Jesus says, "Stop!"' Okay?"

"'Kay."

"Say it for me now."

"Jesus says, 'Stop!'" she murmured.

"Good girl. And after you say that, I want you to think about other things. Don't look at what those bad feelings want you to look at. Think about something happy. Like watching a butterfly flit from flower to flower. Or

Goldie swimming in his bowl. Or your mommy holding your hand as you go for a walk. Can you do that for me right now?"

"'Kay."

Sunshine could see Tessa's features relaxing. Then, before long, amazingly, her breathing evened out and she was asleep.

Grady remained seated on the bed another five minutes, then carefully released Tessa's hand and stood. Wordlessly, they both left the room, Grady quietly closing the bedroom door behind them.

Chapter Fourteen

"You may have to do that with her nightly for a while." Grady moved to the apartment door, his own feelings of tenderness toward Sunshine's daughter leaving him unsettled and ill at ease in the presence of the little girl's mom. "You know, to remind her. To help her make calling on Jesus and thinking about something else a habit."

"I know we're not out of the woods on this, Grady, but I can't thank you enough." Her beautiful eyes reflected her gratefulness. "I'm ashamed, though, that I thought buying her a fish to keep her company would solve anything. That I never recognized that while she knows there's nothing in the closet, she *feels* as if there is."

"Don't beat yourself up. It's an easy enough mistake to make. It's helpful, though, to remember there's no wrong in a feeling itself. God gave them to us for a purpose. But we're not supposed to let them rule us—or control us—in a negative way."

Like running from Sunshine because she, like the woman who'd betrayed him, had a daughter? As Sunshine was doing because she didn't want to be abandoned again, hurt as her ex-husband had hurt her?

She stepped closer, a spark of affection clearly in her

eyes. "How'd you get to be so smart about little girls and things that go bump in the night?"

He chuckled. "My baby sister. When Rio was about four, the son of one of our employees thought it would be funny to lock her in a utility closet. It was only about fifteen or twenty minutes, but after that she was skittish and had trouble sleeping without a night-light. After a few weeks of prayer and guidance, she worked through those fears."

Sunshine tilted her head. "You talked to her like you did Tessa tonight?"

"I can't take credit for that. But that's how my mother handled it, letting the rest of us know so we could reinforce it if we sensed Rio becoming anxious about anything."

"Your mother is a wise woman. But at least she could pinpoint the origin of your sister's fears. I think that would help. I'm at a loss."

"You said this began shortly before school started, so maybe it's related to that? Or something unrelated happened about that time that frightened her? Something's buried there. Maybe you can get her to talk about it now."

"She spent several days with her grandmother—my mom—the week before school started, but Mom didn't mention anything out of the ordinary when I picked Tessa up."

"Something has her rattled. Worrying. And it's manifesting in that closet."

What was he doing anyway, coming across like some renowned child psychologist to a woman who had five years of parenting under her belt while he had zilch?

Leaving the apartment door open so she'd hear Tessa if she cried out, she escorted him down the stairs, then led him through the dim gallery. He paused in front of the faintly illuminated watercolor of Tessa, more reluctant now than before to see it sold to a stranger.

"I'd like to buy this."

Sunshine's eyes rounded.

"Not right this minute. But hold it for me, okay?"

"I'm glad you like it." Her eyes met his in obvious puzzlement. "But I admit this surprises me."

"Why?"

"Because I know that you don't…"

"Don't want to get attached to someone else's kids?" He could give her a song and dance about giving it to someone as a gift, about donating it to an upcoming cancer fund-raiser for a silent auction. But the truth was, he wanted it hanging on his own wall. To be reminded of Tessa. And her mother.

Why did Sunshine have to look so beautiful tonight? Her features softly lit by a faint streetlight coming through the windows. His heart rate ramped up a notch.

"Maybe I was wrong about that." His words came softly. "You know, about the kid thing. There's more to the story and, maybe, I'm…wrong."

"More to what story?"

"The one I fed you last weekend. About the woman I broke up with who had a kid. Yeah, that left me feeling lousy. As if I'd let her daughter down. But even more…"

Sunshine's gaze never left his face.

"Even more, I got hurt because of her betrayal."

"She cheated on you?"

"Not with another man. But she used me—used my family—for financial gain."

Uneasiness flickered through Sunshine's eyes. Obviously he wasn't making himself clear. But how could he explain that mess?

"I won't bore you with the details, but Jasmine was a

successful real estate agent who I'd met through an online photography club. Unbeknownst to me, she was working with clients and their big-time lawyers, wheeling and dealing to get some forest service property deeded to the county and zoned for commercial use."

He could tell by the anxious look on her face that Sunshine still wasn't following. "To make a long story short, she was throwing my name—and that of my family— around as backers of a plan to commercialize a property that we would never have agreed should be commercialized. We're an influential family in these parts, known for our interest in protecting the environment. She was taking advantage of that, playing the odds that no one would come to me for verification when she'd made certain it was widely known that we were seeing each other."

He drew a breath. "When the whole story came out, I learned it was no accident that she'd approached me online to begin with. She'd recognized my name and initiated a chat, which progressed from there. When all was said and done, I ended up feeling as if I'd let my whole family down. And her little girl got hurt, as well."

A stricken look flashed through Sunshine's eyes. "I'm sorry, Grady."

"Thanks. But when you're played for a fool, you can't help but wonder what part was your own fault. If maybe you deserved what you got because you were too stupid to see that you'd let your ego and your too-easily-led-astray heart rule your head."

"You didn't deserve that, Grady." Her words came softly. "You didn't."

"That's debatable. But the point is—" his gaze captured hers "—I've let that betrayal spook me. Let it run my life the past six years. Sort of like Tessa is allowing whatever she imagines is in that closet to control hers.

And—as I suspect—how you're letting that ex-husband rule yours."

He heard a startled intake of breath and reached for her hand. "What I'm trying to say here, Sunshine, is—"

"That you," she offered hesitantly, "like the watercolor of Tessa?"

"I do. And I'd like to buy it. I'd also like…" Heart hammering, he tugged gently on her hand to move her closer, deeper into the shadows. "I'd very much like to kiss you."

Her eyes widened but, not hearing any objections, he leaned in and touched his lips to hers.

Lightly. Ever so lightly. Not daring to ask for more, but savoring the sweet sensation of her mouth on his. Sunshine. So like her namesake, a ray of warmth piercing the icy lock he'd secured on his heart, melting the frozen, off-limits regions he'd allowed to harden over time.

"Grady." Her lips moved softly against his as her hands slipped behind his neck. Drew him closer.

He'd dated a lot of women. Kissed his fair share. But never, ever, had he felt the way he was feeling now with Sunshine in his arms. This overwhelming desire to hold her, cherish her, protect her.

Forever.

Breathless, Sunshine drew back slightly. What was she doing? Not only allowing him to kiss her as she'd never before been kissed, but kissing him back with a zeal she wouldn't later be able to deny.

And she *had* to deny it. Had to convince him they'd gotten carried away in the moment. That it didn't mean anything. *Couldn't* mean anything. And yet… Again she pressed her lips to his warm, inviting mouth as his arms tightened around her.

He'd been betrayed.

Taken advantage of. Hurt deeply. Wasn't she equally as guilty as that other woman? Wasn't she trying to find a way to obtain compensation from the Hunters and, indirectly, from Grady, too?

She drew back again. Found her voice, although it came not much louder than a whisper. A breath. "Grady?"

"So sweet," he murmured as his lips brushed her cheek, obviously loath to let her go.

"Grady. We can't do this."

"Do what?" His gaze met hers, clouded with—what? Surely not love. No, not love.

"We can't—"

"Why not?"

He again touched his lips to hers but, with a willpower she didn't know she possessed, she firmly pressed her palms to his solid chest to gently push him away.

"This won't work, and we both know it."

His forehead puckered as her words sank in. "What are you talking about?"

"Us. You and me. I'm your mother's opponent for town council, or have you forgotten?"

"I can't say that was on my mind these past few minutes, no."

Offering a hard-to-resist smile, he tried to pull her closer, but she resisted, firmly removing his hands from her waist.

"Listen to me, Grady."

"Okay, okay. I'm listening."

He sounded somewhat cross. Which was fine. Maybe his irritation would provoke him into paying closer attention to what she was trying to say.

"Your mother and I are running against each other for a seat on the town council. How do you think your family will feel about me if we start seeing each other? It's a disaster waiting to happen."

Seeing the bewilderment in his eyes, warmth heated her cheeks, flaming hot as realization dawned. Grady hadn't said anything about seeing each other. About dating or love or anything of the kind. He'd only admitted to wanting to *kiss* her.

Which he'd done quite capably.

No wonder he looked confused. Almost dazed. She'd jumped to conclusions. Made a fool of herself.

"Never mind. I think it's time for you to go. I'll have Benton drop off the painting at Hunter's Hideaway. You can give me your credit card number whenever you have time." She grasped him by his rock-solid biceps, attempting to turn him toward the door. But he didn't budge.

"Wait." He held up his hand. "What's going on here, Sunshine? One moment you're kissing me as if there's no tomorrow and the next you're rambling about my family and disasters and trying to boot me out the door. What disasters are you talking about?"

"It's not important. I misspoke."

"What am I not understanding here?" He studied her for a long moment. "Maybe I'm dense, but I thought that not only is there a mutual attraction between us, but that there might be something more substantial."

"Substantial?"

"You know, important. Yeah, physical attraction, but the enjoying each other's company thing, the spiritual bond, too. Maybe something on down the road?" He looked at her doubtfully. "Did I make that up?"

It was tempting to let him think he had. But she couldn't do that to him, especially with relief flooding through her that she hadn't misunderstood the intention of the kiss.

"I do think there's a connection, Grady." As much as she didn't want there to be.

He grinned, and passed the back of his hand across his forehead. "Whew. I thought I was losing it for a minute there. So what's the deal with my family? The disaster stuff?"

"You don't think if we start seeing each other, your family might have a problem with it? And what about Gideon? He already has a target on my back for fraternizing with the enemy."

"The election will be over the second Tuesday in November. A little over three weeks. Then everything goes back to normal."

He took it for granted that Elaine would win. Which she undoubtedly would. "But don't you think—?"

His eyes smiling, he placed a gentle finger momentarily to her lips. "Jesus says, 'Stop.' Remember?"

She laughed, recalling his time with Tessa.

Of course, he was right. The election would be behind them before they knew it. But still…he didn't know about her original intention for coming to Hunter Ridge. What was the likelihood, though, that Tori would find the indisputable evidence she sought? Why not give it up? Let it go? See where things went with Grady?

A murmur of hope rose up in her spirit. Did God have a bigger plan in bringing her and Tessa to Hunter Ridge than simply chasing after some family legend?

"Hey," he whispered. "Tonight Rio and Luke both told me they like you. I think Grandma admires your spunk. Mom feels protective of you. Who cares what the rest of the family thinks?"

"So the rest of your family doesn't like me?"

"Sunshine?" He cocked a brow. "Remember, Jesus says—"

"Stop."

He reached for her hand. "We don't have to make a big deal out of this right now. Nobody has to know where we might be headed when we don't even know ourselves. A few more weeks won't matter. That will give us both time to get used to the idea. Get to know each other better."

He was making sense.

"And behind the scenes—" He wiggled his eyebrows and leaned in close. "We can sneak in a few more kisses."

Laughing, she pulled away. "I think it's time for you to go."

"Just when things are starting to get interesting?"

"For that exact reason."

He let out a disappointed groan. Was this a dream? Grady Hunter was attracted to her? Wanted to get to know her better?

He moved reluctantly toward the door. "Things are going to be crazy this week for both of us. The upcoming election. The grand opening. But I'd like to see you if we can work it out."

"I imagine we could arrange that."

"Good." A quick stolen kiss caught her by surprise.

Laughing at her expression, he slipped into the chilly night. She locked the door behind him and then, with an almost giddy laugh, she crossed the gallery to climb the stairs with a light step. But she'd barely reached the apartment door when the walking-on-air feeling evaporated.

Lord, what am I getting myself into?

Chapter Fifteen

"Your mother isn't up to doing the ribbon cutting at the grand opening tomorrow."

Grady's father rubbed the back of his neck in a weary gesture, then turned back to where he'd been hand sanding splintered wood on the seat of one of the inn's chairs late Friday afternoon. The glare of the work shed's overhead light revealed in his haggard expression the toll concern for his wife was taking.

"She'll rally." Grady adjusted a gooseneck lamp to provide better lighting. Mom had made a decent comeback so many times throughout the chemo treatments. She'd do it again.

"She should be taking better care of herself," Dad said gruffly. "Even with you filling in at the election events, she's overdoing it. Pushing herself."

"That's Mom for you."

"I want her to pull out of the race." Dad reached for a fresh piece of sandpaper. "But she won't hear of it."

"Although she hasn't been able to attend meetings recently, she loves being on the council and wants to fulfill her duties both this term and next."

Dad looked up at him, his gaze bleak. "At what price, son?"

A knot twisted in Grady's gut.

They hadn't dared let themselves consider that she might not come through this. That the chemo wouldn't work. That prayers might be unanswered.

"You know the doc is treating this more aggressively because Mom's mother died from it. There have been promising medical strides since then." The words of assurance were as much for himself as his father. "Mom's going to make it, Dad."

Dad nodded slowly. "She has to. I can't… I don't know how I'd live without your mother, Grady. I—"

His father's voice broke and Grady swiftly moved around the worktable for a quick embrace. "She's going to be fine, Dad."

"We'll be married forty years next June."

"And you'll be celebrating that anniversary together." Unbidden, Sunshine's smile surfaced in his mind. If things worked out as he was beginning to hope they would, could a fortieth anniversary be in their future, too? But loving had a price, as his father was experiencing. "So tell me, Dad, how'd you know Mom was 'the one'?"

Dad returned to his sanding, a slow smile surfacing. "I couldn't stop thinking about her. Couldn't imagine my life without her."

Was that how he was beginning to feel about Sunshine? He sure wasn't getting much sleep at night. All the praying. Wondering how she really felt about him. Remembering every word she said, how the corners of her mouth lifted in a smile, how good that kiss had been.

Dad looked up, studying Grady. "Was that a get-the-old-man's-gloomy-thoughts-diverted question? Or do you have your eye on some young lady? Like that Sunshine gal you spent considerable time talking to on the patio the other night?"

"I—" He wasn't ready to talk about how he felt about Sunshine. He was thinking about her. Spending time with her. But after Jasmine's betrayal, it was like walking on quicksand as he tried to find his footing.

"I know you got handed a raw deal with that other woman a few years back. Took it hard."

"It's not something I'd care to relive." Being manipulated for selfish purposes—left feeling like a fool for thinking she cared for him as much as he did her—wasn't something you easily got over. But Sunshine made him want to try.

"Loving takes courage, son. Risk. There are no guarantees. But don't let the past dictate your future."

The fact that he'd taken her and Tessa to a fun-filled lunch in Canyon Springs on Sunday, talked to her on the phone every night this week and couldn't wait to see her after the grand opening tomorrow had to mean *something*, didn't it?

"How would you feel, Dad, if I did start seeing Sunshine Carston?" There, he'd said it out loud. "I mean, she's Mom's rival and is a vocal backer of the artists in this town, too. There's no getting around either of those facts."

Dad nodded knowingly. "Your mother said she thought there might be something developing there between you two."

"So do either of you have a problem with that?"

He was taking a risk asking a point-blank question. What if Dad said he and Mom didn't like her, that he was making a big mistake? Would that make a difference in his feelings about her?

Dad set aside the sandpaper. "You may not know this, son, but your mother's folks didn't think much of me at first."

"You're kidding." He never would have guessed. But they'd lived in Scottsdale, and Grandma had died when Grady was just a boy, so he wouldn't have been the most perceptive of observers. "Why not?"

"Your mom and I were teenagers when we met, heading into our senior year of high school. Her father had come to the Hideaway to hunt and brought his wife and kids along." Dad shook his head at the memory, a soft smile playing on his lips. "Believe me, I found lots of reasons to hang out wherever your mother might be, which didn't set well with her parents. They were well-to-do and she was college bound. Ivy League. Some punk kid whose folks ran a hunting lodge didn't fit the picture."

"But Mom married you anyway."

"She did. We both knew our own minds. Knew deep down that God had a hand in it. But her folks made the road rocky at first." Dad shifted his weight and looked Grady in the eye. "I guess what I'm trying to say is that your mother and I, we're good with whatever decisions you make as long as you're sure God has a hand in them."

Did God have a hand in his relationship with Sunshine?

It felt right, despite the obvious barriers. But it had felt right with Jasmine, too, hadn't it? No, not like it did now with Sunshine. Sure, he'd been drawn to Jasmine like a moth to a flickering flame. But looking back, it was more of an ego thing. She was smart, beautiful—and he liked how it felt to be seen with her as much as anything. He'd been bowled over by the fact she was into him, a guy from a small town in what most might consider the middle of nowhere.

But a more-than-friends relationship with a spiritual foundation such as the one that was blossoming between him and Sunshine? No, none of that with Jasmine.

"Guess I've given you food for thought, huh?" Dad grinned.

Grady gave him a hesitant smile. "I can't be sure since this is barely getting off the ground. But there's something more there, more solid than what I had with Jasmine."

"Good to hear it."

"This could get sticky, though, you know? Sunshine representing the artists' community and going up against Mom in the election."

"You can't decide who's going to get your vote?" Dad's teasing tone prodded.

Which candidate is it you're campaigning for?

Irvin's question echoed uncomfortably in his head. Dad might find it funny, but it was no laughing matter.

"It's nippy out there, isn't it?" Sunshine shivered as Grady helped her out of his SUV Saturday night, then escorted her up the cabin steps to usher her inside. The scent of baking potatoes welcomed her, triggering a homey whisper of belonging that touched deep inside. Not only of belonging at his place but belonging anywhere he happened to be.

She smiled up at Grady as he assisted in removing her coat, treasuring that quiet, inner assurance. But was she letting her hopes get ahead of her? Despite what Grady had said earlier, she couldn't shake concerns about how she'd be accepted by his family. Their backgrounds were vastly different. She very much wanted to believe that wouldn't matter. But her mother had once alluded to the fact that Sunshine's father's grandfather had pressured him not to marry her, a girl from the other side of the tracks, and instead to wed a woman who fulfilled family expectations. Or was there no substance to that at all, but what Mom chose to believe, unable to face the truth that the man who'd fathered her child didn't love her enough to marry her?

Grady hung her coat on a peg. "I'm glad Tori's back so we could get together tonight. I've missed seeing you. A glimpse or two of you at today's grand opening just didn't do it."

"Unfortunately, she's back because her fiancé broke up with her." Sunshine was both relieved and angered by that turn of events. And no doubt tonight's uncertainty about Grady had been influenced by her friend's emotional upheaval.

"I'm sorry things didn't work out. She's a nice gal." Grady led the way to the dining table, where he had his laptop set up for a final review of his presentation. He'd told her earlier that he liked what she'd developed, so this meeting was probably an excuse to spend time together. Which was fine with her. She'd missed seeing him this week, too, even though she'd delighted in his phone calls.

Late each evening, Tessa having been sound asleep for hours, those moments of intimate conversation filled her with a happiness she'd never before imagined. They'd talked well into the wee hours of the morning, both eagerly sharing hopes and dreams and spiritual journeys. Each generously offering the other a glimpse of who they were as children, teens, young adults. So many questions and a mutual willingness to confide answers drew them closer than she would have expected in such a short time. When had she ever felt so comfortable with a man? So safe in opening her heart without fear of rejection? It was crazy. They'd just met. But in many ways it seemed as if they'd known each other forever.

"Here you go." Grady set a cup of fragrant tea on the table next to her. "This should get you warmed up, and I've lit logs in the fireplace, too. Then as soon as we finish here—I don't think it will take long—I'll throw the steaks on the grill and we'll dine like kings."

"You should have let me bring something. I could have made dessert."

"I have that covered."

"Wow. I feel spoiled."

"You deserve to be spoiled." He settled down next to her and adjusted the laptop screen. "You did a fabulous job on the presentation, putting my data into an eye-catching design."

She took a sip of tea. "You did the hard work. All the research. I got to do the fun stuff. Making it pretty."

"It was your marketing savvy that filtered the research down to something concise and comprehensible." He eyed her hopefully. "I'm thinking it might make sense to have you there when I make the presentation. Not only for moral support, but to field questions. I'll get hammered by Luke and Uncle Doug, and you know this stuff as well as I do now."

"You'll do fine without me there. This is *your* dream, your moment to shine."

"You're my dream, too." His words caught her by surprise as his gaze, smoldering with mischief, drifted to her mouth.

"Now, now, Mr. Hunter." Flustered, she reached over to tap the page-down key, keeping her eyes trained on the next slide. "Let's not mix business with pleasure."

"Where's the fun in that?" He leaned in a tad closer. A ripple of anticipation coursed through her, but she kept her attention glued to the laptop. "Behave yourself now."

He laughed, then settled back in his chair. "Okay, I can take a hint. Let's take a look at this presentation of yours."

She pressed Page Down again with more force than necessary. How absurd to feel disappointed that he didn't persist. That was what she wanted, wasn't it? For their relationship to progress slowly? She was older now, wiser than she'd been when Jerrel had come into her life. With a daughter now to consider, she didn't dare make any mistakes this time.

Not when she might very possibly be falling in love with Grady Hunter.

As they washed up the dishes, Grady couldn't help but occasionally sneak a peek at Sunshine. And each time he did, his heart did a funny little skip he wasn't accustomed to. While he washed and she dried, there were plenty of opportunities for his fingers to brush hers. Or to lean in close to point out which cabinet or drawer an item she'd dried called home. He couldn't remember when he'd enjoyed cleanup chores so much. Maybe he needed to rethink installing a dishwasher his mom seemed to think he should get.

"That was a wonderful meal, Grady." Sunshine looped the damp towel through the handle of the refrigerator. "A perfect ending to your grand-opening day. Were you pleased with the attendance?"

He leaned against the counter. "Actually, I was surprised at the great turnout considering that the largest volume of sales is expected to come from online orders. I guess those merchandise drawings and giveaways for adults and the balloons for the kids did the trick."

"Tessa made me go back three times so she could have one of each color. Red, white and blue."

"Is she sleeping better?" He motioned for Sunshine to precede him into the living room, where they settled in. Her on the sofa, him in his trusty recliner and the fire in the fireplace snapping and crackling and keeping the space comfy.

"It's a little early to tell, but she doesn't seem quite so anxious at bedtime. Sometimes after we've said our prayers and I've left the room, though, I can hear her saying 'Jesus says, "Stop."'"

He couldn't suppress a smile, picturing Tessa, eyes closed and blankets snuggled around her as she told the antagonistic feelings who was boss. "Has she given you any hints as to how this all got started?"

Sunshine shook her head. "None. I'm hesitant to ask if she's not ready to talk about it."

"Give her time."

They were silent for several minutes, both gazing into the flames licking at the logs in the fireplace. He sneaked a look at Sunshine, her gaze thoughtful and...troubled?

Concerned about Tessa?

As if sensing his attention had focused on her, she looked up. "What?"

"Is something besides Tessa weighing on your mind?" Gideon's face flashed into his thoughts. "That Edlow guy isn't causing problems, is he?"

"No more than usual."

"So what's up?"

She brushed the flat of her hand along the sofa's fabric. "This has been such a lovely evening, I hate to spoil it."

A muscle tightened in his chest. Had something he'd shared tonight or during one of those late-night phone calls disturbed her? They'd both shared openly about their pasts, their dreams of the future. He'd never before spoken so freely, so vulnerably to a woman, though. Maybe he'd gone too far.

He let out a slow breath. "There's nothing you can't share with me, Sunshine."

Even if she had something to say that he didn't want to hear.

"I still have some reservations."

"About us?"

She nodded. "I know you said you don't think my running for the town council against your mother is anything to worry about. That it will all be over in a couple of weeks and life will go on."

"But you don't agree?"

"It's not that I don't *want* to agree. It's just that I'm a realist. At least most of the time anyway." She stood and moved to the fireplace, her hands outstretched to the warmth, the dancing flames highlighting her delicate features—and the apprehensive look in her eyes.

He eased himself out of the recliner and joined her, his voice reassuring. "So talk to me."

She turned, tears forming in her eyes. What had he done to make her cry? He reached for her hand. "Did I do something wrong? Say something that hurt you?"

Wiping at the tears with her free hand, she shook her head. "No, not at all."

"What, then?"

"I feel stupid talking about this." She hesitated, composing herself. "What if your parents don't want us to get involved? What if they think I'm not good enough for you?"

"Why would they think that?" He released her hand to cup her face in both of his. "My dad's already told me that he and Mom are good with whatever decisions I make in my life as long as I make sure God's a part of it. And that conversation took place only a few days ago—and in reference to you."

"You talked to them about me?"

"To Dad. So stop with the worrying."

She blinked back tears. "But...he doesn't know that my father never married my mother. I'm illegitimate. Not exactly a prize for you to be carting home to the family."

"Hey, hey." He gently brushed away a tear. "Believe me, nobody's going to hold that against you. That wasn't any of your doing."

"But—"

"God's going to lead us. He'll let us know if this doesn't have His blessing. Wasn't it you who told me that it's His job to close doors? Not mine?"

"Did I say that?"

"I believe so. Therefore, repeat after me. Jesus says...?" He raised a questioning brow.

"Stop," she finished with a giggle, and his heart soared at the sound of it.

Then, before she could avert his intentions, he did what he'd been dying to do all evening.

Kissed her.

Chapter Sixteen

Tori nodded to the envelope Sunshine clenched in her hand. "What are you going to do?"

Sunshine extracted the documents that had arrived in yesterday's mail, still trying to digest what she'd read. "I'm not sure."

"That shows your great-great-grandfather paid the taxes on the property they now call Hunter's Hideaway. I matched the description to land records. The following year Harrison Hunter paid taxes on it. Now I'm searching for a record of sale from your ancestor to Hunter, in case it was a legitimate transfer from one to the other."

"But it could be," Sunshine said softly, "that the Hunters found a way to cheat Walter Royce of his land. Just like Grandma's story."

Tori looked torn, as if unwilling to come to that conclusion. She'd been against this search, this hope that Sunshine had clung to of holding modern-day Hunters accountable. "Documentation can tell half-truths. I'll need to research further, but it looks as if that's a possibility."

"Why didn't he fight it?" Sunshine gave the papers a shake. "Seek legal help? I know Arizona was still a territory, oftentimes lawless, but land grabbers couldn't have been well thought of."

"Didn't you notice the date on the death certificate tucked in there? Not long after he paid the taxes, Walter apparently left this area. The following year he died of pneumonia. That newspaper notice implies he died deep in debt."

Sunshine eased down onto the sofa, overwhelmed by a sudden sadness. "He died and left his family impoverished."

Her family.

A poverty, in fact, that had taken generations to climb their way out of. She clenched her hands in her lap. How different life might have been for her family if Hunter's Hideaway had remained in their possession. If Duke Hunter had indeed paid a fair price for the land that would become Hunter's Hideaway, how could barely a year later her ancestor have died in debt?

"So what are you going to do?" Tori repeated, her tone unsure. "Now that you may possibly have the evidence you want."

"I don't know, Tori. I guess I didn't deep down believe Grandma's story. Didn't think I'd find proof of it anyway." Nor had she foreseen feelings for a man like Grady Hunter would stand in her way if she did find it.

But the dream of righting a wrong was a part of her before she'd met Grady. Before she'd fallen in love with him. Could she march up to the Hunters now and present evidence of their ancestor's duplicity?

A muscle tightened in her stomach. *Betrayal.* That was how Grady would see it. Another betrayal by a woman he cared for. As much as she and Tessa needed a solid financial foundation—their ancient SUV had finally bit the dust yesterday and she had no idea where the next medical-insurance payment would come from—could she do that to him?

And yet…what if things didn't work out between them? The attraction was undoubtedly there. He was a good, godly man, but had she lowered her guard too quickly to dream of what it might be like to share her life with him? To be his wife. To give her daughter a father.

Was that hope realistic? She hadn't dated much since Tessa's father had walked out of her life. A few nice guys had come and gone, but things had never worked out. What if things went no further with Grady than dating relationships had in the past?

No declaration of love. No ring. No wedding.

She glanced uncertainly at the papers in her hand. Were they a God-provided insurance of sorts? If things didn't work out with Grady, could she garner the courage to approach his family? See if they would be willing, out of the goodness of their hearts…?

No. Even if they parted ways, she could never bring herself to hurt Grady like that.

"What am I going to do, Tori?" She gave her friend a determined smile. "Nothing."

Then she crumpled the papers in her hand.

"I've got a bad feeling about this. No offense intended, Grady, but I'm afraid your mother will pull out of the race at the last minute and leave us sitting high and dry." Thin-lipped, Arlen Gifford swallowed down the remainder of his coffee and set his mug firmly on their back corner table at the Log Cabin Café Thursday evening, his expression undeniably gloomy.

Grady cut a look at his uncle Doug, who appeared lost in thought across the table from him. This wasn't the first time he'd heard a similar concern voiced recently and it wasn't surprising to hear it again, even at this impromptu gathering he'd been pulled into by some of Mom's more ardent supporters.

"You can't blame her, Giff, if that's the way it goes." Bo Briggs cut Grady a sympathetic look from under his bushy gray eyebrows. "She looks more exhausted each time I see her."

"She's left us with no options, though." Arlen's tone remained petulant. "If she'd have pulled out a month ago, we could have put someone else forward as a write-in candidate. Now we've missed the registration deadline."

"Don't blame her." Patti Ventura narrowed her black-brown eyes in reprimand. "She'd barely started treatments and couldn't have known how ill they'd make her."

"I'm not blamin', I'm just sayin'."

Bo looked expectantly at Uncle Doug, then Grady. "Are either of you getting a feel for Elaine's plans?"

"I haven't heard one way or another." Grady could honestly voice that. Dad wanted Mom to put her health first. That wasn't for him to share with others, though, not even supporters. Mom and Dad would together make the final decision but, knowing Dad, he wouldn't point-blank tell her what to do.

Uncle Doug folded his arms on the table in front of him. "Elaine won't give up unless she has no choice. I guarantee you that."

Arlen didn't look satisfied with either answer. "I wish we had options, you know? Either Elaine comes through for us, or we're saddled with four years of Irvin or that artist lady."

Dare Grady put in a good word for Sunshine? He cleared his throat to speak, but Bo launched in first.

"Hopefully we can convince her not to forfeit her all-but-guaranteed victory by pulling out of the election."

"But her health, Bo," Patti reminded. "We don't want her taking risks she shouldn't, no matter how much we want her in office."

Uncle Doug rapped his knuckles on the oak table, drawing their attention. Then he glanced almost furtively around the café and leaned in, his voice low. "What if we can get her to hang in there for the election, then resign from office at the opening council session in January?"

He arched a brow, eyes gleaming, and Grady almost groaned out loud. Leave it to Uncle Doug to have a plan. Grandma Jo said that ever since Aunt Char had divorced him, he was always on the alert to avoid being caught off guard again.

"A belated resignation," he continued, not meeting Grady's pointed gaze, "relieves her of council responsibilities to take care of her health, and the city is forced into a special election to replace her."

With a satisfied smile, he settled back into his chair. The others nodded thoughtfully, taking in his idea. Mulling it over.

Would Mom agree to a scheme like that? To deliberately not withdraw prior to the election, knowing full well she intended to resign? It wasn't illegal by any means, but somehow the proposal smacked of not quite right.

"Council rules don't allow for a permanent appointment in her stead," Arlen inserted, "nor would a runner-up from the November election automatically slide into her empty spot. So you're right, there'd have to be a special election."

"Which means," Bo added, "we'd need a candidate the town would rally around. Someone sure to trounce Irvin and that Carston woman if they'd throw their hats into the ring again."

The gazes of Mom's four supporters slid to Grady.

He held up his hands. "Hold on now. Don't look at me."

"You're a natural," Patti encouraged. "You've filled in admirably for your mother, thoroughly know her platform and people are familiar with your face now that you're not buried behind the scenes at the Hideaway. Voters will assume you'll represent them well, just as your mother would."

He chuckled uncomfortably. "I appreciate your faith in me, but—"

"There's been a Hunter on the town council as long as there has been a town council," Bo reminded. "How can you refuse to accept your responsibility to the community?"

His responsibility? Since when?

Uncle Doug rose to his feet and leveled a look down at him. "Hunters have always stepped up to the plate, Grady. Done their civic duty."

Uncle Doug had served several terms himself, but Grady wasn't into politics, wasn't interested in trying to keep an entire town pleased with him. Keeping the Hunter clan happy through the years had been hard enough.

He offered a placating smile. "I think there's plenty of family to keep the tradition going. I'm sure you could talk any one of the others into it."

Patti frowned. "But we want you in that council seat, Grady."

"Thanks, but in all honesty, I don't have time to serve on the town council."

Even with Luke assuming more responsibility, his hands were full. The new business demanded time and attention. Then there was his long-dreamed-of plan to add a wildlife-photography element to the Hideaway's venue. He didn't want to shortchange that, to risk it failing. And what about Sunshine? Would she tackle the special election, too, and he'd find himself running against her?

"We believe you can handle it, boy." Uncle Doug moved to confidently clap him on the shoulder, his voice low but uncompromising. "We want you in that special election—in the town council seat—and we won't take no for an answer. You owe it to your family and to this town."

"Sunshine?"

Grady.

She frantically closed the lid on her laptop and stuffed the folder of telltale documentation underneath it. When Tori had left to take Tessa to the middle-school musical Saturday evening, Sunshine hadn't been able to resist opening her computer on the dining table and taking another look at the photos of Walter and Flora and the burgeoning folder of documentation Tori had accumulated.

Roots. For the first time in her life, she truly had roots. Right here in Hunter Ridge.

But Candy, working late downstairs to set up a special project, had obviously okayed Grady ascending the stairs, not bothering to give her a heads-up. With a quick breath to still her racing heart, she smoothed her skirt, then opened the door to a smiling Grady, who held out a bouquet of cream and bronze chrysanthemums.

"Thank you! I love the autumn colors." She reached for them, then self-consciously spun toward the kitchen to look for a vase. She'd never received flowers from a man before.

"Tessa here?" He glanced around the apartment, then held up a decorative gift bag. "I brought her something, too."

A contented warmth hugged Sunshine. "She'll be back

in another hour. Tori was dying to see a musical she'd helped make the costumes for and borrowed Tessa for the evening."

He set the bag on the counter and watched as she arranged the flowers. "You have a knack for that."

She viewed it from all angles, then carried it to the coffee table in the living room. "So what brings you here bearing gifts tonight?"

"I hadn't seen you in a few days. Although we've talked on the phone, it seemed like a good idea to stop in and make sure you weren't a figment of my imagination." He caught her hand and tugged her toward him, his eyes dancing.

A man who obviously had more kissing on his mind.

She cast him a flirtatious smile. That was all the encouragement he needed, for he immediately stepped in to gently raise her chin with his fingertips and graze his lips across hers. A happy sigh escaped her lips, but before she could slip her arms around his neck he stepped back with a satisfied smile.

"Nope, not a figment. But now that we have that issue resolved, I have something I want to show you." He glanced toward the dining table. "Do you mind if I borrow your laptop?"

Her laptop? With Tori's research folder wedged beneath it and the photo of her and Grady's great-great-grandparents set as the desktop image.

She could explain the photo, though, couldn't she?

"Help yourself." She followed him to the table, where she picked up the laptop and nudged the folder out from under it. Then she lifted the cover and typed in her password. "There you go."

He seated himself, then looked at her with a quizzical

smile. "What do you know? My great-great-grands front and center. You're as bad as my mom about old photos."

"I am. And speaking of your mother, how is she doing?"

His forehead creased as he reached for the mouse, then typed something into the web browser. "Not so good today."

"I'm sorry to hear that." She'd heard speculation around town, people wondering if Elaine would be up to fulfilling her current town council obligations, let alone a future commitment. "Do you think she'll take on another four years?"

Sunshine recoiled from her own words. Did that sound as though she was fishing to find out if she'd have smooth sailing herself with only Irvin to worry about?

"I honestly don't know."

She wanted to ask how his mother was *really* doing and how the family was faring in the wake of her diagnosis. But although her concern for Elaine was genuine, any interest felt two-faced. Intrusive.

"Okay, take a look at this." He turned the laptop so she could see the screen.

A background of subtle autumn colors set the tone, inviting the eye to explore, to take in the striking kaleidoscope of wildlife photographs. When she saw Grady's name in a bold, distinctive font, she gasped. "You have a website?"

"You like it?"

"Oh, I love it." She leaned in closer, acutely aware of his proximity. "You didn't tell me you were doing this."

"I wanted it to be a surprise." He slipped his arm around her waist. "See what an inspiration you are?"

"Your photos are for sale?"

"They are. Or at least they will be when the website

goes live." He clicked on one of the links and guided her through an impressive gallery of elk shots, leaving the other links to be explored. "I've been working with the guy who did the website for the wild game supply store. He's an outdoorsman himself and I think it shows in his design."

"Oh, it does." She lightly touched Grady's shoulder. "I'm so excited that you're doing this."

"I thought you'd be pleased."

"This is why you didn't have as much time as you'd hoped to review what I'd put together for your photography proposal, isn't it?"

"Guilty as charged."

"How's it feel to step out of your comfort zone?" She was proud of him.

He squinted one eye. "Scary?"

Laughing, she leaned in for a hug but, when she straightened, her elbow somehow brushed the folder on the table, pushing it over the edge and strewing its contents onto Grady's lap and the floor.

Heart racing, she knelt to gather the loose papers. But when she stood, breathless, a frowning Grady was examining one of the documents that she'd knocked into his lap. A slightly crumpled one that she'd earlier carefully smoothed out.

Then he looked up at her, confusion in his eyes.

Chapter Seventeen

Grady's stomach lurched as he again stared down at the handwritten name on the photocopied receipt. *Walter Royce*. The ungrateful scoundrel who'd taken advantage of Duke Hunter's generosity. "Where'd you get this?"

"I—" Sunshine's gaze locked with his, her eyes wide.

"Did you get interested in the people in the photograph or something?" He motioned to the laptop. "You do know, don't you, that the guy listed on this receipt is one of the men in the picture?"

She nodded.

He looked down at the wrinkled photocopy again. A tax receipt for land right here in this county. But Walter Royce, to his knowledge, had never owned land around here. Maybe not anywhere. So was this—? It had to be. The infamous receipt for taxes Royce had been sent to pay on behalf of Duke Hunter, who'd been too ill to make the journey himself. A receipt that was written out to the name of Walter Royce.

"Where'd you get this?"

"Tori's been helping me research." She glanced at the folder in her hands.

His gaze held hers, curious. "What were you research-ing?"

"My great-great-grandparents."

That didn't make sense. She wasn't from around here. "What did your great-greats have to do with Walter Royce? No, wait. Don't tell me. He cheated them, too?"

"What do you mean?"

He flicked the paper with the back of his hand.

"This character. He almost cost my great-great-grandparents their land. Fraudulently took out a loan on it, then defaulted." A document like the one he held in his hands would no doubt have been the evidence of own-ership Royce had used to acquire that private loan and purchase a business in a neighboring county. "Did he do your family dirty, too?"

A troubled look wavered in her eyes.

"Sunshine?"

"No, he didn't cheat my family." She swallowed, her eyes riveted on his. "He was—is, actually—family."

"What do you mean?"

"Walter and Flora Royce," she said, her grip tight-ening on the folder in her hands, "are my great-great-grandparents."

It was his turn to stare. "Are you kidding me?"

She shook her head.

"I didn't think you were from around here. Why didn't you say something?"

For a fleeting moment he thought she might not an-swer. Or might bolt. But she stood her ground.

"I didn't have proof of ties to Hunter Ridge, not until you showed me that photograph and told me the names of the people in the picture so I could backtrack to them." The expression in her eyes remained as cautious as the delivery of her words. "I merely had a story to go on that my grandmother shared with me. A story handed down to her about her grandparents who'd lived in an area referred to as the ridge of the hunter."

He'd heard that phrase before. The founders of the town had adapted it when they'd named the fledgling community of Hunter Ridge in the 1920s.

He sat back in his chair. "This blows me away."

In fact, he couldn't get his head around it. The woman he was falling in love with was the great-great-granddaughter of someone who'd almost cost the Hunters their property? Did God have a sense of humor or what?

"Flora," he said softly, studying her. "She was White Mountain Apache. Or at least that's what I was told growing up. That's why you bear traces of Native American ancestry?"

"Considerably diluted, but yes."

"And why you volunteer at that church on the rez? Why Native images play a role in your art?"

She nodded as she placed the folder on the table. "I'm proud of that lineage and want Tessa to be proud of it, too. Working at the church alongside others who share that blood bond gives me a sense of belonging. A sense of my own history, which I knew little of until recently."

"Wow." He shook his head. "I have to admit, this comes as a shock. Not your Apache connection, but your connection to Walter Royce. He's not well thought of in the annals of my own family history."

Her chin lifted. "Wrongly so."

"Why do you say that?"

"You're holding the evidence in your hand." Her words came softly, the look in her eyes a disquieting mix of apology and determination. "It's a tax receipt for the land on which Hunter's Hideaway now stands. Walter Royce owned it, but somehow Duke Hunter managed to disenfranchise Walter and Flora."

That was nuts. She'd gotten the story wrong. "You think old Duke cheated the Royces out of *their* land?"

"My grandmother told me about it when I was growing up, how they'd been swindled. I didn't know what to believe." Her gaze flickered uneasily. "Not until I came to Hunter Ridge to—"

"To what?" He gave a half laugh, trying to make sense of this. "Prove my family cheated your family out of the Hideaway?"

Surely he was misunderstanding. She'd been asked to manage the Artists' Cooperative, right? That was what had brought her here. Brought her into his life. But she didn't laugh, and something deep in his gut twisted at the guilt stamped on her pretty face.

"That's why you came here?" he said softly, an uncomfortable pressure weighing in his chest. "To prove the Hideaway belongs to *your* family?"

Under her startled gaze, he reached for the paper-stuffed folder. Flipped through its contents. Birth certificates. Census and land records. Correspondence. He looked up in disbelief. "Please tell me this isn't what it looks like."

She stood rigidly at his side, her gaze pleading, but she didn't respond.

"All this is an attempt to prove my family stole land from your family?" Having the story wrong didn't excuse the fact that she'd come to Hunter Ridge with an agenda to—what? Hold his family legally liable? To try to wrest the Hideaway from them in court like Aunt Char had attempted when she'd divorced Uncle Doug? To use him and his vulnerable heart to obtain evidence she intended to bring before a judge?

He pushed back in the chair and stood, gripping the folder. Then tossed the paperwork to the table. Hadn't she once admitted that with a child to support, the almighty dollar won out every time? He had to get out of here.

She placed a restraining hand on his arm, finally finding her voice. "Grady, please, I can explain."

"I seriously doubt it." He looked at her, as if into the face of a stranger.

Her grip tightened. "You have to listen to me."

"You're telling me you didn't come to Hunter Ridge with the express purpose of claiming your fair share of the Hideaway?"

"I didn't. Not like that. Yes, I wanted to find out the truth of the family legend, had even hoped that perhaps—"

"Your family never owned a single inch of Hunter property. I can assure you of that."

"But the tax receipt shows—"

"Duke Hunter was seriously ill, Sunshine. He sent a *trusted friend* to pay his taxes. A friend who used that receipt to fraudulently acquire a loan and buy a business. A business that subsequently failed, resulting in a default that brought the authorities and an irate lender to Duke Hunter's doorstep in an attempted foreclosure."

"I don't—"

"Believe it, Sunshine. When your friend continues her research, she's bound to find records documenting the whole thing. Of course, by the time the mess was sorted out, Walter Royce had conveniently gotten himself put six feet under."

She gasped at his insensitive remark, but he continued, "You know what's most sad about that? Duke had plans to deed over to his friend the portion of his property that he'd allowed him and his wife to settle on."

He moved toward the door.

"Grady. Please. You have to believe me when I say I would never have used any of this documentation against your family, even if it was true."

"Never crossed your mind, did it?" His voice sounded harsh in his own ears, but from the look on her face and the absence of a denial, he had no regrets. He reached for the doorknob. "That's what I thought."

"Grady, please. This isn't how it looks. I would never intentionally hurt you or your family. Never try to take Hunter's Hideaway from you. You have no idea how much I—"

"Love me?" He quirked a smile. "Nice try, Sunshine, but that's a bit more than I can swallow right now."

"Grady," she whispered as the door closed behind him with a finality that shattered her heart. Rooted to the floor, an icy cold enveloped her, leaving her shaking.

Once she'd decided not to pursue that avenue with the Hunters, why hadn't she destroyed those papers? Hadn't Tori said it would take more research to confirm what the papers appeared to reveal? She'd told Tori not to do more research. She was done. So why had she given in to looking through the information one last time—and this night of all nights?

If what Grady said was true, that he could prove her great-great-grandfather had never owned so much as a thimbleful of Hunter's Hideaway, that made this even worse.

Sunshine woodenly moved to the table and looked down at her laptop, at the solemn faces on the desktop screen of her great-great-grandparents—and Grady's. Could it be true that Walter—a trusted friend, Grady had called him—had falsely used the Hunter property to acquire a loan? Why would he do that? And how had the story Grandma told gotten so twisted over time?

How long she stood staring down at the vintage photo, she had no idea. A few minutes? Thirty? An hour? But abruptly she was brought back to the present by the sound of feet running up the stairs.

"We're home!" Tessa sounded elated as she burst into the room, but a past-her-bedtime weariness reflected in her eyes. Tori's, too, for that matter, although it wasn't late.

"Let's get you ready for bed and you can tell me all about it."

"What's this?" Tessa, peeling out of her coat, had spotted the brightly colored gift bag on the kitchen counter.

Sunshine handed it to her. "Grady brought you something."

"I missed him?" Tessa's face puckered with disappointment.

"Grady was here, hmm?" Tori gave her a teasing look. "While the kitties are away, the mice—"

"Not exactly."

Her friend's gaze sharpened. "What's up?"

"Later."

"Look, Mommy!" Tessa lifted a stuffed goldfish from the bag, then clasped it to her chest in a hug. "Just like Goldie!"

Still numb, Sunshine knelt to take a closer look at the soft, brightly colored animal. "How cute."

"Grady thinks I'm a good girl, Mommy. Can we call him so Goldie and I can tell him thank-you?"

"Of course he thinks you're a good girl, but it's getting late." She exchanged a glance with Tori. "Let's save that for tomorrow, okay?"

"'Kay." Tessa gave her a hug, then dashed for her bedroom, the stuffed fish tight in her arms.

"That was nice of him," Tori ventured, then tilted her head toward the flowers on the coffee table. "From him, too?"

Sunshine nodded.

"But I get the impression something's not right."

Sunshine drew in a breath and let it out slowly. Could she talk about this right now? Even with Tori? "I guess you'd say we broke up."

Tori's eyes widened. "What happened?"

"He found the documentation of our research." She motioned to the kitchen table. "So he knows everything. About why I came to Hunter Ridge, I mean."

"Oh, Sunshine." Her friend stepped forward to place a comforting hand on her arm. "After you decided to leave the past in the past?"

Sunshine nodded again. "Doesn't hardly seem fair, does it? But he reacted as I thought he might—seeing it as a betrayal. That I was attempting to use him for financial gain like a former girlfriend had."

"You told him, though, didn't you, that you weren't going to use the documentation against his family?"

"I did. But the original intent was there. It couldn't be denied." Sunshine wandered into the living room to look down at the festive flowers. Had it been such a short time ago that Grady had swept her into his arms and playfully kissed her?

"You know what the worst part is?" She cast a bleak look in Tori's direction. "The story that's been passed down in his family is much different than the one in mine. He maintains it was the Hunters who'd been done wrong, not the Royces. That my great-great-grandfather had deliberately made poor decisions that had almost cost them their land. He says he can prove it."

"I did say that additional research was needed." Sadness filled Tori's eyes. "But I'm so sorry. I feel as if this is partly my fault."

"It's not. Don't think that. You were researching what I asked you to research. This was my own doing." All her own doing. "I should have shredded every scrap of paper the minute I decided my relationship with Grady was more important than righting a past wrong."

"You're in love with him?"

"It sure feels like it."

"Mommy! I'm in my jammies!"

"Coming, sweetheart." The ache in Sunshine's chest deepened. Not only had her foolishness driven Grady away, broken her own heart and his, but Tessa would never have the father she deserved and so desperately needed.

"I'll be praying," Tori whispered as Sunshine moved in the direction of Tessa's bedroom. "Praying that once he thinks over what you said, that he'll recognize you hadn't set out to use him."

Inside the cozy bedroom, Tessa cuddled under the flannel sheets, the plush fish secure in her arms.

"Goldie is happy to have a new friend." She lifted one of the toy's soft fins to wave at the fishbowl sitting on the dresser. Then giggled. "I wish Grady could be here to see."

Grady, who only two weeks ago had sat here on the edge of her daughter's bed and prayed with her. Who had encouraged her to say "stop" in Jesus's name to the fears that plagued her. Gradually, ever so gradually, the bedtime anxiety had lessened. Now he'd given her a furry friend to keep her company.

When they'd completed a bedtime story and said their prayers, Sunshine brushed back Tessa's hair and gazed down at her with a love that ached. "Do you want me to leave the night-light on?"

This would be a first if she didn't, but Sunshine could always hope.

Tessa thought a moment, then shook her head. "No. Grandma was wrong."

Grandma? "What do you mean?"

"There's nothing in the closet that will come and get me if I'm not a good girl."

Sunshine's heart stilled. "Grandma told you that?"

"Uh-huh." Tessa frowned at the memory. "When I broke one of her pretty cups she said I was a bad girl. And that bad things came out of the closet at night to get bad girls."

Sickened, Sunshine reached for her hand. Why hadn't she suspected something like this had occurred when Tessa had spent a long weekend with her grandmother before the school year started?

"Why didn't you tell me this, Tessa?"

"'Cause Grandma said if I told anyone, the bad things would come get them, too. I didn't want them to get you, Mommy. Or Grady or Tori."

"Oh, honey." Sunshine squeezed her daughter's hand. "Thank you for wanting to keep us safe, but you can always tell me anything. Always. Promise?"

Tessa nodded. "Why did Grandma tell me bad things are in the closet if it isn't true?"

Touchy ground here, and something she intended to discuss with Mom at the first opportunity. Although she didn't want a distrust built between Tessa and her grandma Heywood, could Sunshine ever trust her enough to leave Tessa alone with her again?

"I don't know. Maybe she was tired that day and made a mistake. Or maybe she was trying to be funny and didn't realize you'd take her seriously."

Or maybe an active five-year-old was too much for her mother these days. Tessa had taken her valuable time and was in her way, much as Sunshine had been when growing up. Never able to keep her mother happy. *Bad girl.* The long-forgotten indictment rang in Sunshine's ears. Maybe the broken cup had upset her mother, but there was no valid excuse for telling Tessa that if she was a bad girl, bad things would get her and those she loved.

"I didn't break the cup on purpose, Mommy. I said I was sorry."

"Of course you didn't do it on purpose. You did the right thing by apologizing." Now Sunshine's mother owed her granddaughter an apology, as well.

"I love you, Mommy."

"I love you, too, sweetie." She pressed a kiss to her daughter's forehead. "So no night-light?"

She shook her head. "Remember? Grady says to think about happy things."

Grady. Their hero.

But what happy things could she possibly find to think about tonight when she turned out her own light?

Chapter Eighteen

"And there you have it." Grady motioned to the wall monitor in a Hunter's Hideaway conference room, then turned to a select group of family members seated around the table. "My proposal for a wildlife-photography addition to our offerings."

Mom hadn't felt up to attending, but Dad and Grandma Jo had joined several of his uncles and aunts. Luke and Delaney. Rio. All had paid respectful attention as he'd gone through the presentation slides. Asked good questions.

But would it be enough?

Would things have gone better had Sunshine been there, lending her support, chiming in on critical points he perhaps hadn't emphasized enough? Maybe she could have helped him refocus when a question from Luke or Uncle Doug had sidetracked him.

"Well put together, son." His father smiled his approval, but his noncommittal choice of words made Grady acutely aware he wasn't ready to deliver a decision.

"This is certainly something to think about," Aunt Suzy said. "Your proposal holds considerable merit."

"I like it," chimed in Rio. "Really, really like it."

He smiled at his little sister, but how much influence would a twenty-year-old have in the final decision making?

Uncle Doug picked up the more detailed backup materials Grady had printed for each of them. "We need time to look over your facts and figures. Luke can run some numbers, then we'll discuss this with you further."

Grady looked to Grandma Jo, questioning.

Her eyes warmed. "It's evident you've put time and effort into this. Your enthusiasm for the project is evident."

So she wanted to look over the numbers, too, think through his proposal.

"I believe it will be worth the time and effort, Grandma." And fun. Something he could sink his teeth into. He could picture the conference room packed with enthusiastic amateur photographers, attention glued to a master photographer guest speaker. Could envision himself overseeing small groups in the predawn stillness of their forested surroundings, helping them capture dreamed-of shots of elk at a watering hole. A deer stepping into a clearing. A hawk soaring overhead.

"Give us time to digest the data you've provided and we'll meet again soon." Dad rose from his chair, the meeting adjourned.

In a now-empty room, Grady shut down his laptop, then deposited it in his office before stepping outside for a breath of fresh air. November already. Fluffy flakes heralding the first snowfall of the season danced before his weary eyes. This autumn had been a season of disappointments in many ways. His mother's medical issues. A delayed commitment on his business proposal. The eye-opening betrayal by Sunshine.

He looked down as something solid bumped almost sympathetically against his leg. Rags. Luke's German shepherd. He knelt down to scratch the friendly fellow behind the ears.

How many times in the past several days had he reached for his phone, hoping that if he called Sunshine she'd tell him he'd dreamed up last week's nightmare? That it had never happened. But he'd be seeing her soon enough, at tonight's last public event before the election. What would they have to say to each other?

He'd been so sure that God was bringing Sunshine and Tessa into his life. How could he have so badly misjudged a woman's intentions twice? And how could she have done this to him, knowing what had happened to him before and how he felt about hurting a child? He hadn't told any of his family members about why Sunshine had come to Hunter Ridge—but should he? He'd need help gathering documentation to disprove her claims if she decided to take them to court.

He gave Rags a final pat, then rose to his feet.

"Grady." Uncle Doug's hand clasped his shoulder. "I'm impressed with your persistence on this wildlife-photography pursuit. I seem to recall you bringing this up years ago. Gave us a good laugh at the time."

Grady gave his uncle a sharp look. "Not so laughable now, is it? When it could be a moneymaker."

"That remains to be seen. But if we can prevent your mother from throwing in the towel for a few more days— which I think we can—your hands will be full with council duties for the next four years. I don't think any of us would be willing to give your proposal the nod, knowing how your time will be limited. A new venture like this will take considerable oversight if it's to succeed."

"You know I haven't agreed to run in a special election, don't you?"

"You will. You'll come through for your family like

you always do. We're counting on you." Uncle Doug clapped him on the back, then, before he could gather his thoughts to respond, his uncle went back inside.

Grady raked his fingers roughly through his hair. No, he hadn't agreed to run in a special election if it came down to that. He didn't *want* to be a councilman. But once again, like many times before, duty called. Family loyalties came into play.

Knowing what he knew about Sunshine now, about her deceptive ways, could he in good conscience refuse to run and leave Hunter Ridge at the mercy of her or Irv?

As Sunshine had also pointed out, with the proliferation of digital cameras, the timing for launching his business plan couldn't be better. Would it still be four years from now? Maybe. Maybe not. Uncle Doug was right—it *would* take tremendous oversight of innumerable details if the endeavor wasn't to fail right out of the starting gate. Sure, the town council only met twice a month, but, as he knew from his mother's involvement, the position involved work sessions, subcommittee meetings and volumes of reading and keeping yourself tuned full-time to the heartbeat of the community's needs and opinions.

Could he turn away from his family's expectations? Let them down? Or would serving his time on the town council somehow make up for his near-miss encounters with two women who'd seen an easy target coming from a mile away?

Was there a chance he could juggle Hunter's Hideaway and the added responsibilities of a wild game supply store, the photography venture and the town council at the same time? Do them all justice?

A heaviness settled into his heart.

Not likely.

* * *

"Four more days, folks." Irvin, having just had his last say in an organized public venue before the election, grinned at Sunshine and Grady as he stepped away from the podium Friday night. "May the best *man* win."

Sunshine managed not to grimace. Surprisingly, Elaine hadn't pulled out of the running, so maybe her health was taking an upward swing. Who'd have known, though, what a big deal a small-town election would be? Not only time-consuming, but physically, mentally and emotionally draining. Did Elaine have it in her to go into another term? And for that matter, did Sunshine have it in her to juggle motherhood, manage the Artists' Cooperative and take on town council commitments for four years?

It was almost with a sense of relief that with Elaine still in the race, she wouldn't have to find an answer to that question. Grady's mother was certain to win.

As the threesome left the elementary-school stage, Sunshine ventured a glance in Grady's direction. He was so handsome tonight that if this were election day and he the candidate rather than his mother, she'd be hard-pressed not to cast her vote on his behalf.

Upon arriving at tonight's event, the two had awkwardly exchanged a handful of pleasantries. Two strangers with nothing to say to each other. Or at least nothing that could be said in a public place. Many times during the past week she'd almost called him to apologize again. But what more could she say to convince him of her sincerity?

She had no intention of asking Tori to research further to prove the evidence one way or another. But she couldn't deny her original plan, the wrong motives that had caused her to jump at the Artists' Co-op position in the first place.

"Sunshine?" Grady's voice drew her attention. "Mom asked me to reaffirm that she wishes you the best in this election and is sorry she couldn't be here tonight to say so in person."

"She's still not feeling well?"

"Conserving her strength for the next four years."

"Please tell her it's been a privilege to share a campaign with her, even though mostly through a very capable proxy." She met his steady gaze with a smile, hoping it might serve as an icebreaker. But he didn't return it. "She's a fine councilwoman, and the town will be fortunate to have her representing them in the next term."

"You're not hoping to win?"

"With your mother running for reelection?" She shook her head. "But it was never about winning. It was about giving a voice to those who didn't have one."

Something unreadable flickered through Grady's eyes. "Then, you've reached your goal before a single vote has been cast."

They stood looking at each other, the conversation coming to a premature close. Was the ache in his heart as heavy as the one in hers? She'd wounded him deeply, if unintentionally. Could she ever make things right with him, even though a shared future wasn't to be? If only so many people weren't milling about, people with whom they were expected to get in a final word that might sway a vote. She had much she wanted to say to him. *Needed* to say.

"We have punch and cookies over here." Mayor Silas urged them forward.

"Coming," Grady acknowledged, but didn't move. Neither did Sunshine.

"Grady," she said, desperate to speak before the moment passed. "I'm so sorry that—"

"I think it's for the best that we not belabor the issue." Sadness filled his eyes—a sadness she'd put there. "I don't hold hard feelings against you. You were doing what you thought you needed to do to provide for Tessa. But we both need to accept that it is what it is and let it go."

But she didn't want to let it go.

"Sunshine! There you are." Local artist Maeve Malone approached, her arms wide to gather Sunshine into a hug. "No matter what happens at the polls, you've drawn attention to the issues surrounding those who don't make their living from the great outdoors. Thank you."

Maeve chatted for what seemed an eternity before disappearing into the crowd once more. When Sunshine turned back to Grady, he'd stepped away, his cell phone pressed to his ear and his expression intent.

"Right. Right. I'll see you shortly."

When he pocketed his phone, he glanced up, looking almost surprised to see her still standing there. Then he swiftly turned his attention to the crowd around them before she could pick up where they'd left off. "I have to leave. Dad's taking Mom to the regional hospital."

"What's wrong?"

"Dad thinks she's dehydrated. Electrolytes or whatever out of balance. Either that or an infection. She wouldn't let him take her earlier today, but now she's giving in."

"I'll be praying."

"Thanks. If you'll excuse me, I need to make a quick round through this crowd, then head to the hospital." He paused, his eyes searching hers. "And, Sunshine—?"

"Yes?" Would he say they needed to talk in private soon?

"Please don't say anything to anyone about Mom and

the hospitalization. They'll probably stick an IV in her and she'll be back on her feet before you know it."

"If anyone asks, I'll say you had pressing Hunter's Hideaway business."

"Thanks." To her surprise, he reached for her hand and gave it a gentle squeeze, then immediately released it.

"Remember, Grady, I'm praying."

Did he recognize what she was saying? That not only was she praying for his mother, but for him, too? Praying God would heal the hurt she'd dealt him and he'd find it in his heart to forgive her even though he could no longer love her?

As he'd predicted, Mom was back home by Saturday afternoon. Prematurely, in his opinion, after seeing Dad help her from the car in what looked to him to still be a weakened state. How long was she going to insist on going through with this election? Were Uncle Doug and her other supporters putting too much pressure on her to hold out until after the first of the year?

As much as he didn't want to run for office, it was his concern for Mom that drove his doubts as to the wisdom of that plan. Was it really so important that a Hunter be on the council, an unbroken chain since the founding of the first one? If he refused to run in the special election—let his family and their friends down—would that provoke Mom into dropping out of the race or would she keep up the fight to remain in office?

He had a night of heavy-duty praying ahead of him.

"You're deep in thought."

He looked up from his desk to see Grandma Jo in his office doorway. "Busy times, Grandma."

"They are indeed." She approached and he rose to pull

up a chair for her. "Your mother is resting comfortably now, glad to be home."

Grandma sat down, but he remained standing. "How long do you think she can keep pushing herself like this?"

"Elaine is a very strong-willed woman."

"At what price?" His words echoed those of his father as he found himself pacing the floor. "Who cares what that council does when she's fighting for her life?"

"I can't argue with you, Grady." Grandma sounded resigned. "But it's not my decision. You know your father wants her to step down, but he won't tell her what to do."

"Maybe he should."

"That's not how the two of them have operated for almost forty years. I imagine you'd like your new friend to drop out of the campaign, too. But are you telling Sunshine to do that?"

He halted his efforts to wear out the carpet. "What she does is none of my business."

"I thought from what I saw at the cookout a few weeks ago and from what your father said recently that there might be a relationship kindling."

"Not anymore."

"Care to talk about it?"

"Not really." But he might need Grandma Jo's help to piece together irrefutable documentation that Walter Royce had never owned so much as the foundation his cabin had been built on. Reluctantly, he moved to shut the door to the hallway, then sat down at his desk once again. "Your grandson's legendary ability to spot a woman taking advantage of him took another hit."

Concern darkened Grandma Jo's eyes, but she didn't say anything, so he continued.

"It's a long story, but almost unbelievably, Sunshine

is Walter and Flora Royce's great-great-granddaughter. You know who I'm talking about, don't you?"

"Of course I do. How extraordinary."

"She came here to prove a story she'd heard from her grandmother—that Hunters cheated Royces out of the property that's now Hunter's Hideaway. She came here not only to prove it, but to cash in on it. And some of the information she gathered to help her she got straight from me. She played me, Grandma, just like Jasmine did."

"I'm sorry to hear this, Grady."

"No more sorry than I am."

"You were coming to care for her, weren't you?"

"Oh, yeah. And her daughter." The hopes and dreams he'd harbored for a too-short time filled his mind. "I can't believe this happened again. What is it about me that tells women I'm a sitting duck to be taken advantage of?"

"The problem isn't you, Grady. It's the women."

"I'd like to believe that, but evidence to the contrary is mounting."

"Sunshine confessed to you, then, that she intends to press the family for money if she can prove this family story?"

"She admitted that's why she moved here in the first place. Of course, she now denies that she'd have gone through with it."

"Do you think she's telling the truth? That perhaps meeting you—even falling in love with you—could have changed her plans?"

"You have no idea how much I'd like to believe that, but it's a little hard to swallow, don't you think?"

"Maybe not. You're a fine young man, Grady. One most women would find it difficult *not* to fall in love with."

Yeah, right.

"She admitted her original plans in coming here. That's a point in her favor."

"After I almost dragged it out of her."

"I imagine it wasn't something easy to admit. We all make mistakes, wrong decisions, but we don't always have to confess them to someone we want to think highly of us."

"You sound as if you believe her."

Grandma rose from her chair to look down at him. "I don't know whether to believe her or not. I just don't want you making a decision based on pride and misunderstanding."

But the decision had already been made.

And after he'd pushed Sunshine away that night, reeling from the blows both she and Jasmine had dealt him, he didn't deserve another chance even if he wanted one.

Chapter Nineteen

"Are you saying what I think you're saying, Grady?" A scowling Uncle Doug, standing among those crowded into Grandma Jo's living room after lunch on Sunday, sounded none too pleased. Undoubtedly he wouldn't be the only one who'd resent Grady's decision once word got out.

So be it.

"I think I've made myself clear," Grady concluded as he looked around the room where he'd gathered his extended family and a few of Mom's closest supporters. "I appreciate your confidence in me and that you believe I'd serve our community well if voted in during a special election. I understand, too, the honor it's been for our family to have had a long, unbroken tradition in Hunter Ridge leadership."

Uncle Doug folded his arms. "You understand that honor, yet you're letting us down."

He didn't want to argue with his uncle. He'd prayerfully made his decision, and nothing would dissuade him. "You can view it that way if you choose to. But I don't think anyone in this room will argue that in the past I've been willing to make sacrifices I've believed to be in the best interests of a family I love. This time, however, I'm being true to myself—and to the God I answer to."

Uncle Doug snorted, eyeing the room to look for those who might share his sentiments. "You're following your heart and sticking this town with the likes of Irvin Baydlin or Sunshine Carston?"

"As always—" Grady refused to sound defensive, knowing what he was about to say wouldn't set well with some "—our family and friends will make their own decisions. But I truly believe that Sunshine Carston will serve this community with fairness and integrity. I encourage you to vote for her. I will be."

As the old saying went, you could hear a pin drop.

With a meaningful glance at Grady's mother—looking fragile this morning, but nevertheless as if a weight had been lifted from her shoulders—Dad rose from where he'd been seated next to her on the sofa. He approached Grady and thrust out his hand.

"Thank you, son. You've made what your mother and I also wish to share that much easier."

What was he talking about?

Dad looked at Grady's mother with love in his eyes, then at those gathered around them. "I'm here to officially announce that Elaine will be resigning from the town council Monday morning—and withdrawing from the election, as well."

Several in the room gasped.

"See what you've done?" Uncle Doug took a step forward, angry eyes fixed on Grady.

"Now, Doug." Dad held up a halting hand to his younger brother. "Elaine and I made this decision last night, before Grady had come to any conclusions of his own. You can't hold him at fault. Blame me and Elaine if you want to blame someone. We decided if God wants her whole and healthy, we're going to do all in our power to keep her that way. And the town council just doesn't fit in the picture."

"I can't believe this." Uncle Doug turned incredulous eyes to Grandma Jo. "Mother? What do you have to say about this? You're just going to let Dave and Grady make this ill-advised decision for all of us?"

Everyone turned to a grim Grandma Jo rising to her feet, and Grady once again admired the regal, almost aristocratic bearing of his grandmother.

"I do have something to say, Doug."

Relief momentarily passed through Uncle Doug's eyes before he shot Grady an I-told-you-so look.

Grandma Jo gave Grady's mother a tender smile, then fixed her gaze once again on her second son. "What I want, Doug, is to keep Elaine with us for as long as God grants us that privilege. If that means the Hunters relinquish the town council seat, then so be it."

"Now, Mother—"

She turned abruptly from Uncle Doug's appeal to look at Grady, her steady gaze filled with love. "Thank you for your courage, Grady. Courage to stand up for what you believe in despite opposition from those you love and admire most. You've not allowed yourself to be pushed down a road where God doesn't want you to go. I love you and I'm proud of you."

Her gaze continued to hold his as he returned her smile.

"Thank you, Grandma. I love you, too."

She'd won.

Still stunned at the news, Sunshine's smile remained frozen following her acceptance speech as supporters cheered and high-fived each other, hugged her and each other. The atmosphere in the restaurant's private room where her campaign team had awaited the election's outcome was euphoric, but standing in the middle of the celebrating crowd, it seemed nothing but surreal. And meaningless. She'd won by default, Elaine Hunter having abruptly withdrawn from the race on Monday morning.

"We did it!" Benton Mason's wife, Lizzie, gave her a hug. "Maybe things will start looking up for the artists in this town."

"I have no doubt," a smiling Benton chimed in, his even white teeth flashing in contrast to his dark beard, "that by next summer an art-in-the-park event will become a reality."

"Hear! Hear!" others around them shouted.

Numb, Sunshine cringed inwardly. She hoped that would be the case. But there were no guarantees. She'd be one voice among five others and Mayor Silas. Half a dozen who might not be pleased to have her in their midst for the next four years. Would people expect more of her than she could deliver? Be disappointed when she might not make a significant difference?

And what about the Hunters? Had the family gotten word of the election results? Were they disappointed that Irvin Baydlin had been beat out by a newcomer?

"Sunshine?"

She stiffened at the familiar voice behind her, then fixing a smile on her face she turned to Gideon Edlow who somewhat reluctantly thrust out his hand.

"I guess congratulations are in order."

"For all of us, Gideon. While I can't make guarantees as to what the next four years will bring, I give you my word that I'll represent the artists and other community members to the best of my ability."

He squinted one eye. "No hard feelings?"

The likelihood that he was done with challenging her and that she'd ever be able to trust him were slim, but bearing a grudge would serve no good purpose. "None."

To her relief, he was apparently satisfied, for he stepped aside to allow other well-wishers in to offer their congratulations.

The remainder of the evening sped by with the mayor and other council members stopping in to offer good wishes and welcome her to the team. Even Irvin came by to concede defeat with surprising graciousness, and Tori allowed Tessa to make a late-night phone call to her mother. Elaine Hunter didn't put in an appearance, but she did make a congratulatory call and explained that it had been a rough day health-wise, which was why she wasn't there in person.

There had been no mention of her son.

It was after midnight before Sunshine, restless and tense, could slip away from the noisy, crowded, too-warm room. In the quiet of the restroom she stared into the mirror at her reflection—into the face of an expressionless stranger. Where was the triumphant, glowing countenance of someone who'd just been elected?

Well, I won, Lord. Now what?

Although Elaine had pulled out at the last minute, her own win hadn't been *entirely* by default. A surprisingly healthy number of votes cast in her favor had by far trumped Irvin's, so at least that meant others outside the artists' community had backed her. Supported her. Clearly, a number of Elaine's supporters had switched loyalties when she'd bowed out, as well.

But although Sunshine hadn't expected to win, the victory felt hollow without Grady at her side. She clearly recognized now that searching for the truth of her grandmother's tale and running for office hadn't been about money or winning. It was about a need to belong. To have roots.

But it wasn't to Hunter Ridge that her soul truly longed to be connected. It was to her Lord. *I am the vine, you are the branches...for apart from Me you can do nothing.*

Reluctantly, she stepped into the dimly lit hallway, the chatter and laughter of those still celebrating coming from the main room. Maybe if she went outside, got a breath of fresh air, the tension that gripped her would ease?

Pushing open a glass door, she exited onto the shadowed porch, grateful for the stillness of this postmidnight hour. It was chilly, but the wind wasn't blowing, and her wool skirt and jacket provided an element of protection.

She moved to the edge of the porch to gaze up at the starry night. At this high elevation, the pinpoints of light glittered more sharply than in lower regions, a breathtaking sweep across the dark expanse above. A reminder of God the Creator, who was in control. A God who still had plans for her—good plans—even though that seemed far from her reality now.

Hey, girl, she chided herself as she rubbed her hands up and down her arms to warm them, *you won a seat on the Hunter Ridge Town Council.*

That had to be a God thing, didn't it?

But, ungratefully, it wasn't enough. If only she could go back in time and rearrange her life. Purify her motive for coming to Hunter Ridge and abandon the selfish pursuit to unearth the truth about the Hunters and her great-great-grandparents before she'd even gotten started.

Stop herself from hurting the man she loved.

"Sunshine?"

Startled, she spun toward Grady as he stepped up on the far side of the shadowed porch.

"I was hoping to see you. To offer my congratulations." His words came hesitantly. "But I wasn't sure if I'd be welcome."

"You'll always be welcomed, Grady." Always. But how stupid to have said that. As if expecting him to casually brush off the deep wound she'd inflicted. "I'm more sorry than you'll ever know. I understand why it's difficult for you to believe it, but I never intended—"

He held up his hand to halt her. "I know that now."

A spark of hope flared as he moved closer, but she tamped it down. It would be too much to bear if he'd solely come here tonight to seek closure. To say a final goodbye.

He looked down the concrete porch and scuffed the toe of his boot against it. "We've both grown up with different versions of the same story, haven't we?"

"We have."

"You wouldn't think that something that happened a hundred years ago would trickle down through the generations to impact us now. Influence who we are. But I know for my part, I grew up with tales of how my ancestor generously supported a friend facing hard times and was taken advantage of. Then when Uncle Doug's wife divorced him and did him and the town dirty when I was a little boy, well, that was another layer of distrust and fear of betrayal that carved itself into who I am."

"And then Jasmine."

"Yes, and then Jasmine." He looked skyward for a long moment, then back at her. "But you've been impacted by a story, as well. An often-told story shared with you by someone you loved and trusted—your grandmother. A tale that, as with me, seeped inside and planted itself in how you perceive the world. As betraying. Untrustworthy. And your ex-husband's abandonment reinforced that."

"It did."

"I guess what I'm trying to say here is that we both blindly walked into a relationship carrying a ton of personal baggage. Heavy baggage we weren't fully aware we were carrying until now. Some of it with century-old roots."

"Kind of crazy."

"Major crazy." He raked his hand through his hair. "I'm confident, Sunshine, that the evidence you've discovered can easily be explained. That it can be proved beyond a shadow of a doubt that your great-great-grandfather never owned Hunter's Hideaway. But I don't expect you to take my word on that. I'm willing to research it further with you and, if the Hunters did your family an injustice, we'll make it right."

"I don't want anything from the Hunters." Except Grady's trust, his heart. "Please believe that."

"I believe you'd come to a decision that you wouldn't press my family for financial gain. I've thought long and hard about what you said or, rather, what you were trying to say when I refused to listen. When I was being stubbornly sure you were no better than Jasmine. Than Aunt Char. Than your ancestors."

Despite his assurance that he believed her, she cringed inwardly at the string of past betrayals carving a path into his future. Was it any wonder he'd reacted the way he had?

"But God—and Grandma Jo—opened my eyes, Sunshine."

"Your grandmother?"

"That's a story to be told later." He reached for her hand, his gaze intense. "I had to ask myself if something that happened or didn't happen a hundred years ago to people long dead even matters. To us, I mean. Here. Now."

"Only if we choose to let it."

He swallowed, his hands tightening gently on hers. "Will you forgive me, Sunshine? For not believing in you? I can see now that my betrayal of you was every bit as harsh as the one I'd imagined inflicted on myself."

"Of course, Grady. But I owe you an apology as well, so please hear me out. My original motives for coming here were wrong. Very wrong. I was intent on being compensated for an injustice done to my family—an injustice I'd clung to so tightly, but now realize was a fabrication."

The lines of tension in his face eased.

"I now also realize," she hurried on, "that coming here and then running for a town council seat wasn't all about money or fighting for justice. Those things masked a search for the fulfillment of another deeper need. A need for roots, a sense of belonging. But this past week I've come to better understand that true belonging can only be found by not withholding pieces of my heart from God."

The stillness of the night pressing in around them, they stood facing each other in the dim light. Despite words of reconciliation and a desire to put the past in the past, he'd said nothing of wanting to see her again. To start over. Was it too late for that?

"Grady, I—"

"I have something I need to say first." And then, as her heart leaped into her throat, he dropped down on one knee to look up at her, his hands still holding hers. "I know this is coming out of the blue. That it might be premature. That you might think it's downright crazy. But I love you, Sunshine. Tessa, too. And I want to spend the rest of my life with both of you. Will you give me a second chance? Will you marry me?"

Heart pounding, she stood staring down at him, trying to absorb his unexpected declaration. *Grady loves me. He wants to marry me.*

"I understand," he said, almost stumbling over his words, "if you can't give an answer right now. But would you be willing to think it over? To pray about it—as I've done?"

He thought she needed more time?

"I don't need to think about it any further. I've prayed about it, too."

Uncertainty flickered through his eyes. Then he swallowed, as though steeling himself for a turndown. Did he have no idea how she felt about him? How for weeks she'd dreamed of someday hearing him utter those words? How thrilled Tessa would be?

"I love you, Grady Hunter," she said softly, "and, yes, I will marry you."

He stared at her, uncomprehending. "You—?"

She laughed. "I love you. And Tessa loves you, too."

He blinked. Once. Twice. Absorbing her words. Then an uncontrollable grin surfaced and he rose swiftly to his feet to gaze down at her, still speechless.

"Cat got your tongue?" she coaxed playfully.

With a laugh, he slowly shook his head, his eyes filled with wonder. "You've made me the happiest man in the world, Sunshine."

"And you'll—hopefully soon—be married to the happiest woman in the world."

He gently cupped her face with his warm hands. "I do love you, Sunshine, and I promise to make you a good husband. And Tessa a good father."

"I don't doubt that for a moment."

Grady chuckled. "I'm not sure how God managed this. We did our best to botch up His plans, didn't we?"

"We did."

"So I guess we need to show Him our appreciation and make up for lost time." With that declaration and a twinkle in his eyes, he leaned in to tenderly press his lips to hers.

Epilogue

❧

"It's beautiful, Grady." Sunshine held out her hand to admire the glittering diamond ring, her breath coming as a frosty cloud on the crisp mid-November morning air. Returning from an exhilarating forest hike, they'd paused at the edge of Hunter's Hideaway property, where they'd soon join Tessa, Tori and Grady's family for an engagement celebration brunch.

How quickly her life had changed. Whoever would have imagined what God had in mind when she'd come to Hunter Ridge, determined to uncover the truth about her great-great-grandparents? She'd never have guessed what He had planned the day she'd brazenly marched up to Grady, demanding he call off the noisy workers next door. Whoever would have thought she'd win a council seat and her assistance would help Grady receive unanimous approval to pursue his dream of a wildlife-photography element at Hunter's Hideaway? Or almost unanimous. She didn't count his uncle Doug's dissenting vote.

"That ring isn't half as beautiful as you are." Grady leaned in for a lingering kiss, then gently tugged her leather glove back on. "If you keep taking that glove off, your fingers are going to turn into blocks of ice."

"I'm not worried." She slipped her arms around his scarf-wrapped neck. "Isn't it your job to keep me warm now?"

"You think so, huh?" His eyes twinkled as he pulled her close. Or as close as they could get with them both wearing down-filled jackets. "I believe I can handle that assignment."

She cuddled into him. "I'm glad we won't be waiting until next summer to get married. Valentine's Day is perfect."

"I wish it could be Christmas. Or Thanksgiving." He gently rested his forehead against hers. "But hopefully, if the chemo finally begins to work its wonders, Mom will feel up to enjoying the wedding by February."

"She still has long way to go, doesn't she?"

"More treatments. More meds. More physical therapy. But, God willing, next year she and Dad will celebrate their fortieth wedding anniversary together, and then each year thereafter for a long time to come."

"I think she's relieved not to be facing another four years on the town council."

"I get that impression, too—that pulling out of the campaign took a lot of pressure off her." His gloved finger touched the tip of her nose. "Thanks to you."

"Me?" She laughed. "Oh, right. I challenged her for the council seat and won by default. I'm sure it's going to take your folks a while to forgive me for that."

"They're grateful. Especially Dad. Mom never would have withdrawn if she didn't think you could beat Irvin. She'd have kept pushing herself, wearing herself out."

She tilted her head. "She thought I'd beat him?"

"Hands down. And look how it's turned out." He arched a brow. "The town council seat remains in the Hunter family. The tradition unbroken."

"Ah, but don't forget." She lifted her chin with mock defiance. "I'll be representing the artists in the community, too, you know. Not just Hunters."

"I know that, and I'm proud that you will be." He again captured her lips with his and, with a quick intake of breath and pounding heart, she returned the kiss, marveling that God had given her—and Tessa—a man like Grady Hunter.

"Hey, you two!" Guiltily jerking apart at the sound of a gruff voice, they looked across the clearing to where Pastor McCrae stood at the back patio door of the inn, motioning them forward. "There's plenty of time for that lovey-dovey stuff later. Get yourselves on in here. Time to eat."

"Spoilsport!" a grinning Grady taunted back at his cousin, then reached for Sunshine's gloved hand. "So are you ready to officially unveil that ring? The whole family will be in there by now, waiting to see it."

The *extended* Hunter family. Consisting of many who might not be thrilled that she'd won the election instead of Elaine. Who might be less than thrilled that she was marrying into the Hunter clan, claiming Grady as her own.

"Once they get to know you, they're going to love you." He'd guessed what was on her mind. "Just as I do."

Then, before she could protest, he leaned in to again move his warm lips gently on hers. She could barely keep her knees from buckling or from throwing herself into his arms.

"Hey!" Garrett called again, amusement evident in his tone. "What part of 'bacon and eggs getting cold' don't you two understand?"

Sunshine giggled and Grady drew back, shaking his head. "I never knew a preacher could be so annoying."

Gazing up into Grady's warm blue eyes, she linked

her arm with his. "I guess we'd better not force him to come out here after us, huh?"

He sighed. "Guess not."

With her free hand, she reached up to touch her beloved's face, her words coming softly. "I love you, Grady."

"I love you, too, my very own Sunshine."

Smiling, they headed toward the inn—and a lifetime shared together.

* * * * *

Dear Reader,

Welcome back to Hunter Ridge! I loved writing Grady and Sunshine's story—the journey of two wounded hearts learning to trust God so He can enable them to overcome past betrayals and learn to love again.

It's a rocky road at times. Not only do they have their personal pasts to overcome, but their lives are uniquely entangled with others who have come before them—both in the recent and distant past.

Have you ever felt betrayed by someone you trusted? Did it impact your ability to trust others? Or perhaps made you so fearful of letting others down that you haven't always listened to and obeyed God's direction? Never forget that one of the beauties of a relationship with God is that He tells us "never will I leave you, never will I forsake you."

You can contact me via email at glynna@glynnakaye.com. Please visit my website at glynnakaye.com—and stop by loveinspiredauthors.com, seekerville.net and seekerville.blogspot.com!

Glynna Kaye

COMING NEXT MONTH FROM
Love Inspired®

Available May 24, 2016

HER RANCHER BODYGUARD
Martin's Crossing • by Brenda Minton

To keep Kayla Stanford safe, bodyguard Boone Wilder decides to hide her amongst his family in Martin's Crossing. Watching her care for his ill father, Boone realizes there's more to the free-spirited socialite—she may just be his perfect match.

THE AMISH MIDWIFE'S COURTSHIP
by Cheryl Williford

Tired of her mother's matchmaking, midwife Molly Ziegler asks her family's boarder Isaac Graber to fake interest in her. As their pretend courtship turns to real love, can they see past what's make-believe and find real happiness together?

LAKESIDE SWEETHEART
Men of Millbrook Lake • by Lenora Worth

Teaming up with local minister Rory Sanderson to mentor a troubled teen, Vanessa Donovan is soon confronted with her own painful memories. Can Rory help her heal and show her she's worthy of a future—with him?

THE COWBOY MEETS HIS MATCH
Rodeo Heroes • by Leann Harris

Working with Sawyer Jensen to revitalize the local rodeo, Erin Delong never expected the stubborn cowboy to be so open to her ideas—or that he'd be the man to get through the barriers around her heart.

FALLING FOR THE HOMETOWN HERO
by Mindy Obenhaus

When he hires Grace McAllen as the office manager for his new business, former soldier Kaleb Palmer is only looking to rebuild the company's reputation. He hadn't counted on the pretty brunette being the only person who could help mend his wounds.

SMALL-TOWN NANNY
Rescue River • by Lee Tobin McClain

Becoming a summer nanny allows teacher Susan Hayashi a chance to financially assist her family. But when she clashes with the little girl's widowed millionaire father, can they reconcile their differences and see they're meant to share a happily-ever-after?

REQUEST YOUR FREE BOOKS!

2 FREE INSPIRATIONAL NOVELS
PLUS 2
FREE
MYSTERY GIFTS

Love Inspired®

YES! Please send me 2 FREE Love Inspired® novels and my 2 FREE mystery gifts (gifts are worth about $10). After receiving them, if I don't wish to receive any more books, I can return the shipping statement marked "cancel." If I don't cancel, I will receive 6 brand-new novels every month and be billed just $4.99 per book in the U.S. or $5.49 per book in Canada. That's a saving of at least 17% off the cover price. It's quite a bargain! Shipping and handling is just 50¢ per book in the U.S. and 75¢ per book in Canada.* I understand that accepting the 2 free books and gifts places me under no obligation to buy anything. I can always return a shipment and cancel at any time. Even if I never buy another book, the two free books and gifts are mine to keep forever.

105/305 IDN GH5P

Name	(PLEASE PRINT)	
Address		Apt. #
City	State/Prov.	Zip/Postal Code

Signature (if under 18, a parent or guardian must sign)

Mail to the **Reader Service:**
IN U.S.A.: P.O. Box 1867, Buffalo, NY 14240-1867
IN CANADA: P.O. Box 609, Fort Erie, Ontario L2A 5X3

**Are you a subscriber to Love Inspired® books
and want to receive the larger-print edition?
Call 1-800-873-8635 or visit www.ReaderService.com.**

* Terms and prices subject to change without notice. Prices do not include applicable taxes. Sales tax applicable in N.Y. Canadian residents will be charged applicable taxes. Offer not valid in Quebec. This offer is limited to one order per household. Not valid for current subscribers to Love Inspired books. All orders subject to credit approval. Credit or debit balances in a customer's account(s) may be offset by any other outstanding balance owed by or to the customer. Please allow 4 to 6 weeks for delivery. Offer available while quantities last.

Your Privacy—The Reader Service is committed to protecting your privacy. Our Privacy Policy is available online at www.ReaderService.com or upon request from the Reader Service.

We make a portion of our mailing list available to reputable third parties that offer products we believe may interest you. If you prefer that we not exchange your name with third parties, or if you wish to clarify or modify your communication preferences, please visit us at www.ReaderService.com/consumerchoice or write to us at Reader Service Preference Service, P.O. Box 9062, Buffalo, NY 14240-9062. Include your complete name and address.

LI15

When Kayla had discovered she had a bodyguard, she
hadn't expected this. He should be in the background,
quietly observing. Her father was a lawyer and a
politician; she'd seen bodyguards and knew how they
did their jobs. And yet here she sat with this family, her
bodyguard talking of cattle and fixing fence as his sisters
tried to cajole him into taking them to look at a pair of
horses owned by Kayla's brother.

A hand settled on her back. She glanced at the man
next to her, his dark eyes crinkled at the corners and his
mouth quirked, revealing a dimple in his left cheek.

Boone opened his mouth as if to say something but
a heavy knock on the front door interrupted. He pushed
away from the table and gave them all an apologetic look.

"I think I'll get that." His gaze landed on Kayla. "You
stay right where you are until I say otherwise."

"They wouldn't come here," she said. And she'd meant
to sound strong; instead it came out like a question.

"We don't know what they would or wouldn't do,
because we don't know who they are. Stay." Boone

walked away, his brother Jase getting up and going after him.

Kayla avoided looking at his family, who still remained at the table. Conversation had of course ended. She knew they were looking at her. She knew that she had invaded their life.

And she knew that her bodyguard might seem like a relaxed cowboy, but he wasn't. He was the man standing between her and the unknown.

Don't miss
HER RANCHER BODYGUARD
by Brenda Minton, available June 2016 wherever
Love Inspired® books and ebooks are sold.

www.LoveInspired.com

LIEXP0516

Reading Has Its Rewards

Earn **FREE BOOKS!**

Register at **Harlequin My Rewards** and submit your Harlequin purchases from wherever you shop to earn points for free books and other exclusive rewards.

Plus submit your purchases from now till May 30th for a chance to win a $500 Visa Card*.

Visit **HarlequinMyRewards.com** today

MYR16R1